baby girl

MEMORY HOUSE SERIES, BOOK FOUR

BETTE LEE CROSBY

BABY GIRL
Memory House Series, Book Four

Copyright © 2016 by Bette Lee Crosby

Cover design: damonza.com
Formatting by Author E.M.S.
Editor: Ekta Garg

ISBN: 978-0-9969214-2-8

BENT PINE PUBLISHING
Port Saint Lucie, FL

Published in the United States of America

OTHER BOOKS BY THIS AUTHOR

For Crystal J. Casavant-Otto

I will be forever grateful to you for
sharing a story that took hold of
my heart and never let go.

CHERYL ANN FERGUSON

When I left Spruce Street, I was crazy in love and thought I knew exactly where I was going. Life, despite its ups and downs, was stretched out in front of me like one long highway to happiness. I discovered soon enough that there are forks in the road, places where the path splits off in two different directions and you're forced to choose one way or the other.

There are no signs on this road, no arrows pointing this way for Happy Ever After and that way for Years of Regret. You choose blindly and trust your heart will take you in the right direction. It doesn't always.

I chose many of the wrong roads and now have a storehouse of both memories and regrets. There were times when I loved and times when I hated. I did both with a passion so fierce it tore holes in my heart.

Now I have at long last reached my destination. I am where I was meant to be. Those much wiser than me claim that no matter what pathway a person chooses, in time they will end up where they were intended to be. I have reached a point in my life where I believe this is true.

To understand this journey, you'd have to know how it all began some twenty-odd years ago.

1991

The first time I laid eyes on Ryan Carter was the day he and his mama moved into the Ballinger place. The house had stood empty for three, maybe four years and was considered an eyesore even for Spruce Street.

Rumor had it that Alfred Ballinger bought the house with intentions of fixing it up, but he died just three months after they moved in. The whole three days he was lying in a casket waiting to be buried, his wife, Martha, sat by his side. Then once he'd been laid to rest she went back to the house and closed the curtains, and that was the last anybody ever saw of her.

According to Mama, Martha Ballinger was just waiting to die, but it took almost twenty years to happen. In all that time not a single repair was made to the house. It sat there with the paint peeling and the shutters hanging loose. When the lawn got to be knee high, one of the neighbors generally came by with a lawn mower or weed whacker and cut it back.

The Ballinger place is only two doors down from us, so we were among the first to catch hold of the stench. It was in the early spring when Mama flung open the windows to air the house out. After two sniffs, she knew something was wrong.

"Felix, get outside and check the backyard!" she screamed. "There's a dead animal stinking up the place."

Daddy went looking and traced the smell to Missus Ballinger's house. He knocked at the door for more than twenty minutes, and when nobody answered he banged out a pane of glass and climbed in the window. That's when he found her, dead as a doornail.

There was no telling how long she'd been there. Since there were no friends or family to call, the county came and carted off her body. With no mortgage on the house and no relatives looking to claim ownership, it sat there getting more dilapidated year after year.

Mama said not in a million years would they be able to sell that place, but as it turned out she was wrong.

IN LATE JULY, ON A day that was considerably hotter than it should have been, I spotted the U-Haul truck rounding the corner at the far end of Spruce Street. It was moving slow like a lost dog in search of a place to settle.

Spruce Street wasn't a place where people cruised by to look at houses or cut through on their way to someplace else. It was just two short blocks with wood frame houses on both sides and little strips of yard in between the houses. Seven doors down from us the street turned to a dead end. Once you passed by the Gomez house that was it. The only thing you could do was make a three-point turn and drive out the same way you drove in.

Mama and I were on the front porch trying to cool down. I squatted on the steps, and she was pushing herself back and forth in the swing.

"Looks like some damn fool has got himself lost," she said.

"Maybe we're gonna get new neighbors," I replied wistfully.

Mama gave a cynical grump and fanned her face with the postcard from Aunt Mildred. "That ain't likely."

The U-Haul slowed to a crawl once it crossed Jenkins Road

and came to a rolling stop when it passed our place. The woman in the driver's seat craned her neck to see the number on our mailbox then moved on.

"Lord God," Mama said with a groan, "I do believe those idiots are headed for Martha Ballinger's place."

The Ballinger place was the only vacancy on Spruce Street. Sure enough, two doors down the truck creaked to a stop.

RYAN CARTER WAS FIRST TO step out of the truck. He gave a long lazy stretch then combed his hair back with his fingers. He was the kind of guy you couldn't help but notice: good looking with a chiseled jaw and dark hair that tumbled onto his forehead. He was wearing a black tee shirt with something written on the front, but he was too far away for me to see what it was.

I watched as he came around to the back end of the truck and raised the door. He climbed inside, shoved a few boxes onto the loading platform, then jumped down and started carrying them to the house.

His mama tromped up the walkway ahead of him, unlocked the front door, then disappeared inside. She was twice the size of Ryan and bristly from head to toe. It was obvious she had little patience for anything not to her liking. I could hear her fussing at him.

"Get your butt in gear," she said with a grunt. "We don't have all day!"

It seemed the more she fussed the slower he moved, almost like he was trying to aggravate her, although why wasn't obvious. Twice she raked him over the coals good and proper, and both times he gave a satisfied grin and walked off with a swagger.

Mama and I both had our noses turned toward the Ballinger place. The hedge around that house was nothing but a few bare branches sticking up out of the ground, so from our front porch you could see and hear most everything.

On his third trip back to the truck, Ryan glanced over and caught me looking at him. He kind of nodded and gave me a wink. I didn't want him to know I'd been watching, so I lowered my eyes, started picking at a scab on my knee and pretended not to notice. When he went back to carrying boxes, I went back to watching.

NOTHING EXCITING EVER HAPPENED ON Spruce Street. Absolutely nothing. To have somebody moving in or out was big news, and Mama liked to be first with gossip of any sort. She watched everything Ryan carried in, and when he went by with a mahogany nightstand she murmured, "Looks like they've got halfway decent furniture. Wonder why they'd pay good money for a rundown old house?"

I shrugged. "I don't know."

Since Mama wasn't about to help carry boxes and couldn't come up with any reason for going over there herself, she swatted me on the back of my head and said, "Instead of sitting here being useless, get yourself over there and lend a hand."

"Okay," I answered and jumped up.

The minute I stepped off the porch, I saw Ryan eyeing me. When I strolled up the walkway and told him I'd come to lend a hand, he gave me a grin and said he thought I might.

Years later I would think back on that hot summer day and remember him hot and sweaty with his tee shirt stuck to his skin and that sexy grin calling out to me. I think that's when I fell in love with him.

THAT AFTERNOON RYAN AND I carried in all those boxes, plus several pieces of furniture. While we were unloading the U-Haul we laughed and joked as if we'd been friends forever. A big kitchen table was the last thing to come out of the truck. Ryan pushed it to the edge of the loading platform and yelled, "Hey, kid, get the other end of this, will ya?"

Kid. That's what he called me. He had two years on me, but I was nearly as tall and looked older than my age.

"I'm no kid," I said. "I'll be fifteen in three months."

He laughed. "Three months, huh?"

I nodded.

"Okay, so how about I call you kid for the next three months, then I'll switch over to Cheryl Ann?"

"How about you just call me Cheryl and start right now?"

He grinned, and it wasn't the kind of grin he gave his mama. This one was sincere. I could feel the warmth of it taking hold of my heart.

"So, Cheryl," he said, "you gonna get the other end of this table or not?"

THAT'S HOW IT STARTED. WE became friends, and our mamas did too. Blanche Carter and Mama had a lot in common. They both saw life as one giant thing to complain about.

For the rest of that summer, Missus Carter was at our house almost every day. She'd amble down about a half-hour after Daddy left for work and stay for hours. Mama would brew a fresh pot of coffee and they'd sit at the kitchen table, Missus Carter talking about the no-good husband who'd left when Ryan was just a baby and Mama talking about Daddy.

According to Mama, Daddy had next to no ambition, was lazy as a log and snored like a sick bull. Mama told every bad thing she could think of, but she never once mentioned how Daddy made people feel good about themselves and happy to be around him.

Once when Missus Carter was in the middle of complaining about Ryan's daddy, Mama said, "Blanche, consider yourself lucky. Having no man is better than having one who's worthless."

Her words were clear as a bell. Even though I was in the living room, I heard them. Hearing Mama imply Daddy was worthless made me come as close as a person can come to hating someone. I loved Daddy with all my heart. She might have thought him worthless, but to me he was the dearest person in the world.

When Mama would start picking at me, Daddy would almost always step in.

"Cheryl Ann's got more than her share of good qualities," he'd say and give me a hug right there in front of her. Afterwards he'd take me to Wilke's Drugstore for ice cream. We'd sit in a booth across from one another, drinking sodas and talking.

"It's not because your mama doesn't love us," Daddy used to say. "She's just high strung and lets aggravation get to her. Your mama's the sort who takes her troubles to heart."

There were times when I thought Mama didn't even have a heart, but I never said so. I wanted Daddy to think I was forgiving like him instead of being judgmental like Mama.

FOR THE REST OF THAT summer when Mama and Missus Carter settled at the kitchen table with their coffee and complaints, I'd slip out the back door, go down the block and help Ryan fix up their house. By the time school started we'd cleared the weeds out of the yard, nailed the shutters back in place and painted the whole downstairs.

I know it sounds like a lot of work, but it wasn't. When you're doing something with somebody special, work doesn't feel like work. I liked Ryan. A lot. I liked when he high-fived me or bumped his hip up against mine. I liked when our hands touched and when we sat together on the back step. In a way that's hard to explain, being with Ryan was like being with Daddy. He made me feel good about myself and happy to be near him.

Two Years Later

The year Daddy died everything changed. It happened two weeks before Thanksgiving on a Saturday that started out just like any other day. Mama was fussing because of the leaves in the yard.

"Our yard doesn't look one bit worse than any other house on the block," Daddy said patiently. "The oaks lose their leaves every year, so why get riled up over something that's inevitable?"

Mama gave a loud harrumph, then slid Daddy's eggs out of the frying pan while they were still runny. She picked up the plate and thumped it down in front of him.

"I'm expecting that yard to be cleaned up today," she snapped.

With Mama there was no mistaking a command. She made it perfectly clear that if you didn't do what she said, there would be hell to pay.

Daddy saw those slimy eggs swimming in a pool of grease and pushed his plate back. He finished his coffee then got up from the table.

"Well, I guess I'd better get started," he said, and those were the last words he ever spoke.

An hour or so later I was up in my bedroom and heard a thud.

I stuck my head out the window and looked down into the backyard. There was Daddy lying face down with the rake still in one hand.

He died before they got him to the hospital.

UNTIL THAT DAY MAMA NEVER had a kind word for Daddy, but once he was gone she became the most sorrowful woman in town. When the neighbors stopped by with casseroles and pies, she'd sit in the living room chair and dab at her eyes.

"I don't know how I'll manage without Felix," she'd say with a moan. "I've got nothing to live for."

That's what I was to Mama—the same as nothing. She and I never did have a good relationship, but after Daddy was gone it went from bad to worse.

He once told me Mama had a bitter attitude toward life because of what happened with her sister, Gilda. He said Granny Keller had Mama late in life, so between a sister who was twelve years older and parents who were already up in years Mama was spoiled from the get go. Whatever she asked for she got, and if she didn't she'd throw a hissy fit. When everybody got weary of listening to her scream and cry, they'd give her what she wanted just to hush her up.

"Why'd you marry Mama if she was so spoiled?" I asked.

Daddy gave a sad little smile and said, "Because I fell in love with her. Once you fall in love with somebody you keep loving them, even if they've got faults."

According to Daddy, Mama was sixteen when Gilda got married and moved to London. Going off and leaving her behind was something Mama never could forgive. She refused to answer Gilda's letters or even speak her name. Two years later Gilda and her husband were both killed in a car accident, and Mama never got over it.

"It's not that she doesn't want to love you," Daddy said. "She's afraid to."

I asked how he knew all that stuff, and he said Granny Keller told him the year before she died.

⟨◎⟩

WITH DADDY GONE IT WAS just Mama and me, and we didn't have much to say to one another. After a few weeks of eating dinner in silence, Mama bought a little TV and set it on the kitchen counter. That's how we ate dinner every night, Mama with her eyes glued to the television and me listening to a Sheryl Crow or Mariah Carey cassette on my Walkman.

I can't begin to count the number of times I cried myself to sleep that year. I'd wake up in the morning and get dressed for school with my eyes all red and puffy. It got to the point where even Mama noticed how bad I was looking.

"What's wrong with you?" she asked. She suggested maybe I ought to stop in and let Doctor Simpson take a look at me. Not once did she consider that maybe all I needed was a big old hug like Daddy used to give me.

That year I walked to school by myself every day. Ryan had graduated the previous spring and now had a job working in Mike's Automotive Shop. He also had a car and a girlfriend, so I seldom saw him. It was as if I'd lost both Daddy and Ryan that same year.

I tried to get back to some semblance of a normal life, but with Mama it was impossible. In mid-December when every store in town was blinking red and green Christmas lights, I asked if we could have a small tree.

"Just something to brighten up the house," I said. "Make it seem less gloomy."

Mama looked at me like I'd gone stark raving mad. "Have

you no sensitivity? Can't you see I'm a woman in mourning?"

Oddly enough Mama seemed to be enjoying her mourning way more than she'd enjoyed life with Daddy. As long as she continued to walk around dabbing at her eyes the neighbors showered her with sympathy, and that was something she reveled in.

That Christmas I used my babysitting money to buy her a nice new robe. When I gave her the robe, instead of saying how happy she was to have it she said, "How can you think of gifts when my Felix is lying dead in the ground?"

Mama seemed to have forgotten that her Felix was also my daddy.

Christmas morning we went to the cemetery together, said a few prayers at his grave, then went home. That afternoon was the same as every other day. We sat across the table from one another eating ham sandwiches, Mama watching the TV and me listening to music on my Walkman.

After it got dark I went for a walk by myself. Being alone on the dark street was comforting in a way. I could let go of the misery inside of me and didn't have to explain it to anybody. That night I pretended Daddy was walking alongside of me, telling me to dry my tears and be patient with Mama. I knew it was the kind of thing he'd say if he were still here.

With school closed until January 3rd, that was the longest and most miserable week of my life. That Thursday I walked down to Ryan's house thinking maybe we could hang out but Miranda, his girlfriend, was there, and she was hanging on to him like he was the last man on earth.

He asked if I'd like to go to the movies with them, but I said no. I didn't want to be a third person tagalong. I wanted to be Miranda.

I CAN'T SAY IF LIFE got better with Mama or I got used to living the way we were, but by the end of the school year we'd stopped looking daggers at each other. Mama eventually gave up her role as the grieving widow and went back to being her old cantankerous self.

Without Daddy to remind her that I did have some good qualities, she started finding fault with everything. My skirt was too short. My hair was too long. I didn't sit straight. I had a sassy mouth. Her list was endless. Even when I tried to be pleasant, she'd say I had an attitude that was not becoming of a lady.

The only person Mama didn't find fault with was Blanche Carter. Neither of them saw the faults in each other, but once they'd parked themselves at the kitchen table with a full pot of coffee they could tell you everything that was wrong with the rest of the world.

THE DAY SCHOOL LET OUT I went down to The Produce Basket and got a job working the cash register. I loved that job. It got me away from Mama and put money in my pocket. I saved most of what I made and added it to the college fund Daddy set up for me.

On the Fourth of July, The Produce Basket was closed. Mister Barnes said not to bother coming to work because everybody in Back Bay would be picnicking or getting ready to watch the fireworks.

Needless to say, Mama and I weren't doing either.

That afternoon when we were eating lunch at the kitchen table, I asked Mama if we could go to the fireworks together.

"I've got no time for such foolishness," she said.

I argued it was just one evening and she'd have a good time, but it was like talking to a stone wall.

Daddy was the one who loved fireworks. Every Fourth of July he used to take me to the town square. We'd bring a blanket and sit in the grass. He'd buy us two bottles of soda pop; then we'd lean back and watch the sky light up. While the fireworks exploded in bursts of red, white and blue, the high school band played *Yankee Doodle Dandy* and a bunch of other songs. At the end they'd play *God Bless America*, and everybody would stand up and sing along.

Remembering how it was made me miss Daddy more than ever. I squatted on our front steps feeling miserable and watching the sky turn dusky when Ryan pulled up in his convertible with the top down.

"Whatcha doing?" he asked.

Missing Daddy and the fireworks had put me in a bad mood, so I gave him a short answer.

"What's it look like? I'm sitting here doing nothing."

"The fireworks are gonna start in a half hour," he replied. "You'd better get a move on."

"I'm not going."

"Why not?"

I was in no mood for beating around the bush. "I don't have a car, and Mama won't take me."

"If you wanna go, I'll take you." He smiled and gave a nod toward the passenger seat. "Come on, hop in."

"Oh, yeah, I'm sure Miranda would *love* to have me tagging along."

"Miranda?" He laughed. "We broke up two months ago."

"Give me five minutes to put on some lipstick," I said and dashed into the house. In two minutes flat I had tugged on my new white shorts and pink tank top, brushed some lip-gloss on my mouth and was out the door.

I still remember that ride to town with the wind blowing through my hair and the smell of Ryan's after-shave tickling my nose. For the first time since Daddy died I was happy. Truly happy.

The square was already crowded when we got there. Ryan parked on the far end of town, grabbed a blanket from his car and looped his arm across my shoulder as we tried to find a spot.

After walking around the square three times, we finally found a narrow strip of grass between Wilke's Drugstore and the parking lot. That's where we spread the blanket.

When the fireworks started I scooted close to Ryan the same way I used to do with Daddy. He looked down, gave me a sly grin, then wrapped his arm around my waist and tugged me even closer. Before the evening was over, I was flat on my back and Ryan was kissing me just the way I'd always wanted.

YOU CAN'T LOVE SOMEONE WITH your whole heart and keep parts of yourself from him, so I suppose it was inevitable. But it was different than I'd imagined. I'd always thought one special night we'd go out for an elegant dinner with wine and dancing, then check into a fancy hotel, and there, in a room with brocade draperies and plump pillows, we'd make love.

Instead it happened on an August night when the daytime temperature had skyrocketed past 102. The air in our stuffy little house was almost too hot to breathe. I was dressed in a pair of skimpy shorts and a camisole with no bra. When Ryan beeped the horn in front of the house, I ran out and jumped in the car.

Fanning my hand back and forth in front of my face, I said, "Let's go."

He stepped on the gas, and minutes later we were breezing along Cascade Avenue. He drove around for fifteen or twenty minutes; then we stopped at the roadhouse on Route 9 and ordered icy cold mugs of beer.

Afterward neither of us was in the mood to go back to the sweltering heat of Spruce Street, so he drove to Lookout Point and parked. The night air felt good against my skin, so I reclined my seat and looked up at the stars.

"I wish we could stay here forever." I sighed and closed my eyes.

I expected Ryan to kiss me but didn't expect he'd already have his shirt off. The feeling of his bare skin against mine aroused a passion that shot through my body like an electric current. One moment we were kissing, and then before I knew what happened he'd slid his hand inside my camisole and climbed astride me. I should have stopped him right then, but it was already too late. I wanted him as much as he wanted me. Perhaps I'd sound less trashy if I said I tried to fight him off, but the truth is I didn't. I gave myself willingly.

After that first time there was no more holding back. Night after night we'd go off and make love in the backseat of his car. I told myself what's done is done, and besides it wasn't just a physical thing. We were in love. Truly in love.

We even had plans to get married. I had one more year of high school and then two years at the junior college. So we'd continue to live at home, save our money and get married when I finished college. That was the plan, and at the time it seemed we had all the bases covered.

On warm summer evenings we'd walk through town arm in arm as if we were already married, sometimes pretending we were the Mister and Missus Carter who lived in the charming six-story condominium building on the corner of Grant Street and Hightstown Boulevard. We'd already decided our first big purchase would be a house, either a cute little cape cod or a condominium in that building on Grant Street.

This is how the dream went; we'd get settled in our own place and keep right on saving. In another year or two we'd have enough money for Ryan to open his own automotive repair shop.

LOOKING BACK I ASK MYSELF if it was ever really my dream or if I was simply swept up in loving Ryan. Of course, it's impossible to look back and see things as they were because your perspective changes depending on where you stand. If you don't believe me, try it yourself. Move from one side of a room to the other and see if things don't look different. What was once big and bulky now seems small, and the tiny thing that warranted no attention has suddenly become the focal point.

This type of distortion is even more pronounced when you move forward or backward in time. In the blink of an eye time can shrink a span of years down to something that would fit on the head of pin, and you're left wondering how it happened.

Although a number of years have passed and there are a million small things I've forgotten, the one thing I remember about that year is that it was one of great happiness. I belonged to Ryan, and he belonged to me. Back then I thought I could never wish for anything more.

GRADUATION 1995

By the time Mama finally broke down and got a Christmas tree, I was a senior in high school. It was the first tree we'd had since Daddy died. For two straight years she'd refused to have one. The first year she claimed it would be a disgrace to Daddy's memory, and the second year she said it was too much damn work.

If Mama had her way we wouldn't have had a tree that year either, but Ryan showed up at the door with a six-foot Frasier fir. Had it been anyone else she would have tossed him and the tree out into the yard, but Ryan was Blanche Carter's boy and that made all the difference in the world.

On Christmas Eve Mama roasted a small turkey and invited the Carters to dinner. We ate in the dining room for the first time in years, and she let me play my Johnny Mathis Christmas tape. With the music playing, Ryan cracking jokes and Mama laughing, it was almost like it used to be when Daddy was alive.

After dinner Ryan and I cleared the table and did the dishes. Then we headed out for the midnight church service. Mama and Blanche Carter stayed behind; they'd already settled at the kitchen table with their mugs of coffee.

It doesn't snow much in Virginia, but that night there were

flurries. Not enough to stick to the ground but enough to make it feel Christmas-y. I was wearing my new red scarf pulled up around my neck. Ryan and I walked side by side, his arm tight around my waist and our hips brushing against one another every third or fourth step.

At the Christmas Eve service there was no sermon, just the choir singing songs of praise and a reading from the Bible that told of Jesus's birth. At the end they dimmed the lights, passed out candles and lit them from one another. When everyone lifted their candles into the air, the lights were turned off. The organ was silenced, and the only thing to be heard was the sweet clear voice of a woman singing *Silent Night*. After the first two lines, the choir director motioned for us to join in and we did.

Standing beside Ryan in that candlelit sanctuary, hearing all those voices mixed together in happiness and praise, I felt anything was possible. It was a new world, a world of love and hope and goodness.

That night Ryan gave me an engagement ring and officially asked me to marry him. We'd already talked about it, but the ring was a surprise. It was a pearl with a tiny diamond on each side. The ring probably cost less than a hundred dollars, but once he slid it on my finger it felt like a five-carat diamond.

THE FOLLOWING MARCH I FILLED out an application for Bay River Junior College. They had a good dental technician program, and if I graduated it was almost a guarantee of getting a job for thirty-five thousand or more. Although an essay wasn't mandatory, I wrote one and included it with my application. My marks were good, not great, but I stood a pretty fair chance of being accepted.

For almost two years I'd taken the money I made at The

Produce Basket and from baby-sitting and added it to the college fund Daddy set up for me. I had almost four thousand dollars. It was all in that savings account with just my name and Daddy's name on it. Mama wasn't listed, and that riled her to no end. At least a half-dozen times she'd suggested that with him gone her name ought to be on the account. I'd thought about doing it just to appease her but remembered Daddy saying this was strictly between him and me.

THE ACCEPTANCE LETTER ARRIVED IN May, two weeks before graduation. When I got home from school it was lying on the hall table. Opened. I read that I'd been accepted and let out a happy whoop.

It was obvious Mama had already seen the letter, but I was excited and didn't take time to think. I hurried through the house and found her sitting at the kitchen table the same as always, her fingers wrapped around a half-empty coffee mug and her face puckered up with a look of aggravation.

That look was nothing out of the ordinary, so I ignored it and shouted, "I made it! I've been accepted to Bay River!"

Without changing her expression one iota, she said, "You're not going."

When a roller coaster crosses over the highest trestle then starts down, there is a moment when it feels like you've fallen through the floor; well, that's what this felt like.

"Not going?" I said, stunned. "What do you mean not going?"

"It's time you got a job and contributed to the upkeep of this house," she said. "All these years I've been—"

"Mama," I said sharply, "I plan on getting a job soon as I finish college. A dental technician makes good money and—"

"There's not going to be any college. I'm not spending what little bit of money I've got—"

"You don't have to pay anything. I've already got my tuition saved up."

She snorted. "Enough for a year maybe; then you'll have your hand out looking for more."

A swell of anger rose in my chest. "I don't need your money! I've got my own money, the money Daddy left me!"

I guess the thought of Daddy and me sharing something that didn't include her got stuck in Mama's craw, because she turned mean as a snake.

"Okay then, Miss I've-got-my-own-money sassy mouth, let me put it to you this way. You either get a job and start paying for your room and board, or you can find yourself another place to live!"

Pushing back my anger, I tried to answer in a civil tongue.

"You don't mean that," I said. "You know Daddy intended for me to go to college."

Mama stuck her nose in the air and turned away.

"I don't know anything of the sort," she said. "That was something you and your daddy never shared with me."

Without another word, she emptied the dregs of her coffee down the drain and left the room.

Mama and I never did get along real well, but I don't think I ever hated her as much as I did at that moment.

FOR THE REMAINDER OF THE day we didn't speak to each other. I went to my room, slammed the door, then laid on my bed sobbing.

That night when Ryan came to pick me up, it was obvious I'd been crying. My eyes looked like two big red strawberries.

"What's wrong?" he asked.

"Mama's not going to let me go to college," I said.

He shook his head as if he couldn't believe his ears.

"Wait a few days," he finally suggested. "I bet she'll come around."

DURING THE NEXT TWO WEEKS, I went out of my way trying to be nice to Mama. I made certain my room was spotless clean, and after dinner I'd jump up and clear the table before she had a chance to mention it. Several times I asked if she'd given any further thought to my going to college, and she turned away as if she hadn't heard me.

When I handed Mama the ticket to my graduation, she laid it on the sideboard and went back to what she was doing.

I reminded her of it the morning of my graduation.

"The ceremony starts at four o'clock."

"The time's on the ticket," she replied with a frosty air. Seconds later she asked, "Have you decided what you're doing after graduation?"

Caught up in the excitement of the day, I answered, "Yes, we're going to a party at Barbara Miller's house."

She gave me a look of pure hatred and snapped, "You know that's not what I was asking about!" With the words still hanging in the air, she turned on her heel and stomped out of the room.

Mama made it obvious she was mad at me, but I didn't think she'd be spiteful enough to skip my graduation.

At four o'clock sharp the ceremony started. I looked out into the audience and saw the chair next to Ryan was empty. That empty chair felt like the weight of the world pushing against my chest. When Principal Browning called my name, I had tears streaming down my face. By then I'd made my decision.

THE APARTMENT

Two days after graduation I packed my bag and left. Mama was sitting at the kitchen table when I passed.

"Goodbye, Mama," I said, but she didn't even look up.

When I stepped outside Ryan was already waiting for me. We drove to Burnsville that afternoon and stayed in a twenty-nine dollar a night motel on the interstate.

You might think with that being our first time actually spending the night together we would have made wild passionate love, but we didn't. I couldn't get the image of Mama's angry face out of my mind and kept crying. Ryan sat beside me and rubbed my back.

"I know you're scared," he said, "but we're gonna do just fine. We're not giving up our dreams, we're just taking a different path to get there."

"But we have nothing," I said, sobbing.

"Sure we do," he said. "We have each other."

I wanted him to understand how brokenhearted I felt because I didn't have Mama anymore, but after I thought about it I realized I never did. Neither Daddy nor I ever had Mama. We had each other and she had us. We were the story of Gilda written in a different handwriting.

It was well past midnight before I finally drifted off. The next morning we got up, got dressed and started looking for an apartment.

We had the money I'd set aside for college, but it had to last until we got on our feet so we took the cheapest place we could find. It was a three-room flat above a delicatessen. We paid the first month's rent in cash then moved in with nothing but two suitcases.

That afternoon we drove over to Downing, found the Salvation Army Thrift Shop and bought furniture for the apartment. Everything, including a worn plaid sofa, an oak table with two chairs and the bed, came to a grand total of three hundred and twelve dollars.

"Newlyweds?" the silver-haired woman at the register asked.

I nodded. We weren't married but we planned to be, so it seemed a harmless enough lie.

"You're going to need more than just furniture," she said. "Have you got sheets? Towels? Kitchenware?"

I shook my head. "Not yet."

"Well, here, let me help you." She took my hand and led me to the side room where the rows of tables were piled high with merchandise. Grabbing two large boxes from beneath the table, she walked down one row and up the next.

"You'll need accessories for the bathroom," she said and plopped a stack towels in the first box. "And dishes and flatware."

"I don't know that we can afford—"

"We don't just sell things here," she said, turning to me. "We give things away too. These things are donations. Someone gave them to us, and now I'm giving them to you." She smiled and continued down the row. "And sheets; you'll need sheets and pillows and blankets…"

As I followed behind her I couldn't help but wish she were my mother.

23

"Do you have any kids?" I asked.

"No." She shook her head ruefully. "I always wanted to have one but…"

I was tempted to say, "You can have me because my mama doesn't want me," but I didn't. It was a silly thought. Just wishful thinking.

WE LOADED THE TWO CARTONS into Ryan's car and headed back to the apartment. The truck would deliver our furniture the next day.

It's funny how certain moments stay in your head forever. I remember how happy we were that night. We bought a loaf of sour dough bread and a container of soup from the delicatessen downstairs and ate dinner standing at the kitchen counter. Afterward we fixed a bed on the floor and made love.

We'd made love hundreds of times before, but it was never quite like that night. With our Salvation Army furnishings and the future stretched out in front of us like a ripe promise, I thought this was everything I could ask for. That night I slept with my head on Ryan's shoulder and the thump of his heartbeat beneath my hand.

TWO DAYS LATER RYAN LANDED a job working the counter of an automotive parts supplier. It was five days a week plus double time on Saturdays if he was willing to work. At the end of that first week when he got his paycheck, he bought a six-pack of Budweiser and a pound of roast beef from the delicatessen. That night as we settled at our second-hand table eating thick roast beef sandwiches and drinking beer from the can, it felt like a celebration.

"I'm figuring I'll work two Saturdays, then we can buy a TV," Ryan said. "And once you get a job we'll go back to saving for a house."

"Yeah, once I get a job..." The rest of my thought was left hanging in the air because I'd discovered finding a job wasn't as easy as I'd thought it would be. Without the two years of junior college, the only thing I had to offer was typing.

It took me almost two weeks to find a job, and when I finally did it was working in the classified ads department of the Burnsville *Tribune*. I made six dollars an hour answering the telephone and helping people write ads for things like used cribs or exercise equipment.

"Tribune Classifieds," I'd say cheerfully, then copy down whatever they wanted to sell, rent, give away or buy. I was only one of six girls working the classifieds. Nicole Polanski sat next to me, and she was the one who taught me how to make the most of my day.

"Go for the up-sell," she said. "If your ratio is more than 75 percent, there's a bonus."

An up-sell was talking a customer into running the ad for a week rather than just two or three days.

"Tell them it's $2.80 a day if you run the ad for a week," Nicole advised, "and $4.20 a day if you do just two days."

"But won't that cost more money?"

"Not really," she said and gave a devilish grin. "You can save the customer money by using abbreviations."

She showed me how to turn a listing for an elegantly landscaped three-bedroom house with a new kitchen, playroom and two-car garage into "Scenic 3BR + den, new appls, dbl gar." Before long I had an 85 percent ratio and was collecting a bonus every week.

By then Nicole and I had become fast friends. We ate lunch together every day and shared the down and dirty secrets of our life.

She's the one who helped me move past feeling guilty about Mama.

"When a person gives you nothing but misery," she said, "then it's time to move on and find happiness. It's always there, but sometimes you've got to do a lot of looking to find it."

The thing I liked about Nicole was that she'd offer a piece of advice then move on. She didn't keep harping on the same thing over and over again the way Mama did.

Three months after I started working the classifieds, Willard Moss, the advertising manager, called for me. Willard was a white-haired no-nonsense man who did a bullet-shot walk from the elevator to his office, never glancing right or left.

I was working on an ad for a garage sale on Clancy Street when Sheila, the floor supervisor, tapped me on the shoulder.

"Willard wants to see you in his office," she said.

Out on the floor we laughingly referred to him as Willard, but if we had occasion to come face to face it was always Mister Moss.

"What for?" I asked nervously.

She shrugged. "How would I know?"

I turned my computer monitor off and started down the long hall. I was thinking *Please, God, don't let this be that he's letting me go.* I began reviewing the past three months and realized perhaps making the up-sell bonus every week wasn't such a good idea after all. Hopefully it wasn't something that warranted firing.

Maybe the paper is cutting back, trimming the fat, so to speak. I was the last person hired, and if they were laying people off I'd be the first to go.

The door of his office was open, but I tapped on it anyway.

"You wanted to see me, Mister Moss?" I asked, my voice as timid as that of a squeaky mouse.

He looked up from the papers he'd been reading and nodded. "Come in, and pull that door closed behind you."

Oh, crap, I'm getting laid off.

I sat, straightened my back and folded my hands in my lap.

When your stomach is doing flip-flops, there is no way to look casual or comfortable.

"I've been keeping an eye on the way you work with customers," he said, "and I think you're wasting your time here."

"Actually I really like this job," I cut in. "I like helping people and—"

Before I could finish telling him how happy I was in the job, he said, "I need somebody with your ability working outside. I'd like to move you into space sales. I won't lie, it's a commission job so you'd get less money to start with, but with your personality I think you could double your income in a month or so."

I gasped. "Double my income?"

"Maybe even triple it!"

THAT EVENING I TOLD RYAN about my new job and said I'd need to borrow his car because I had to go from place to place to call on the businesses. He was none too crazy about the thought of my using his car and liked it even less when my first paycheck was half of what I'd been making.

"This is just a draw against the commissions I'll be making," I said. "By next month it should be more."

He eyed me with a scowl then turned away. "Hopefully."

That night I made up my mind. Come hell or high water, I was going to make a success of myself in this business.

THE THIRD MONTH I RECEIVED my first big commission check, more than double what I'd been making. Before year-end I was earning as much as Ryan most every month, and some months I was making more. By then he'd gotten me a 1987 Chevrolet Caprice.

Life was good. We now had a fully furnished apartment, two cars and a brand new television.

NEW LIFE

It's funny how having a few good things in your life can cause you to turn a blind eye to problems loitering in the shadows. While there was no doubt Ryan and I would eventually get married, we weren't rushing it. For now we were both happy, and that was enough.

On the few occasions when I mentioned marriage, Ryan turned it off by saying we first needed to get ourselves "established." Instead of talking about marriage, we spoke of other things. The things he wanted. A house, a new car and now he'd added a boat to the list.

"Wouldn't it be fun to have a nice little cabin cruiser?" he said. "We could dock it on the James River and join the yacht club. There are parties every weekend; imagine the fun we'd have..."

With his words he painted a picture of happiness. At night we'd lie in bed, my head resting against the curve of his chest and him telling of the places we'd go and the things we'd do. Without ever once objecting, I let his dreams settle in my head and become mine.

ONCE OR TWICE A WEEK Nicole and I met for lunch, and I'd rattle on about all the plans Ryan and I had. She was happy for me but not as happy as I was for myself.

Every so often she would ask when we were getting married and I'd answer, "As soon as we're established."

In time this caused her to tilt her head and give me a grimace of doubt. She'd once told me Ryan had the look of trouble attached to him, but after that the only thing she said was, "Be careful."

Nicole and Ryan didn't hit it off; knowing that, I brushed past her warning without giving it a second thought.

When the time is right we'll get married.

FOURTEEN MONTHS AFTER WE MOVED to Burnsville, Ryan and I bought our first house. It was a fixer-upper with a back porch that needed replacing, but it was cheap and could be had with a minimal down payment. In a heartbeat we went from being two carefree kids camped out atop a delicatessen to being homeowners.

Ryan traded in his slick convertible and got a one-year-old truck, a Dodge Ram that had 16,000 miles on it. Instead of going to the movies or having dinner at the Chinese restaurant in the evening, we hurried home and worked on fixing up the house. Almost every week we spent Saturday morning at Home Depot stocking up on another load of hardware and paint. On the way there we'd circle around the drive-through, grab a coffee and egg McMuffin, then be waiting at Home Depot when the store opened.

It was fun holding paint swatches next to one another, picking out the perfect beige for the living room, then moving on to finding tiles for the kitchen or handles for a cabinet. We'd take a cart and go from aisle to aisle in search of whatever we needed: nails, hooks, a claw hammer, an electric screwdriver.

Each week it was something different, but once the truck was loaded we'd hurry home and start working. I'd be right alongside of Ryan, hammering, painting, cleaning gutters and digging weeds out of the yard. It was like the early days when he and his mama first moved to Spruce Street, only now we weren't fixing up her house. We were working on a place of our own. Some afternoons we'd turn the radio to a music station, push up the volume and sing along as if we were at a music festival.

When we finished working we'd shower together, then fall into bed and make love. When Ryan held me in his arms and whispered how much he loved me, I couldn't imagine wanting anything more.

THE THING ABOUT TROUBLE IS that you seldom see it coming. You're moving through life with everything looking rosy, so you don't bother to question what's ahead.

Willard Moss, pleased with sales, expanded my territory and gave me the six towns surrounding Burnsville. This doubled my income but made for a long day with few breaks. I was on the road before seven in the morning and more often than not worked straight through until seven in the evening.

This routine had its ups and downs. The upside was that I felt better about myself than I'd felt in a very long time. I was the *Tribune's* top space salesperson, an equal partner in our house and had whittled myself down to a size eight, which was the thinnest I'd ever been. The downside was that my life was moving at 100 miles per hour, and there was no way to slow down. I seldom had time for lunch because there was always another client to call on.

Success is a cruel master. The more you have, the more you want. Day after day Ryan pushed me to want more. It was a carrot he held out, and I kept running after it. In the evening when we lay side by side in the bed, his words would breathe life into that oh-so-tempting carrot.

"Just think of it," he'd say. "If we keep going like we are, in a year or two we can buy a bigger house with a swimming pool. At night we can swim naked and…"

He described everything: the marbled foyer of the house, the blue tiles of the pool, even the waterfall that would cascade from the hot tub into the pool. Listening to him I could see the clear blue water surrounded by tall hedges of boxwood. I could hear the echo of our laughter and feel the passion of what came afterward.

"Before long we'll be able to afford a boat," he said. "I'm thinking maybe a twenty-six-foot cruiser with a cabin below deck. We'll keep the fridge stocked with cold beer, and on hot summer nights we'll motor out into the bay, drop anchor and make love. Afterward we'll just lie there letting the waves rock us to sleep."

As he spoke I could picture myself in a bikini that showed off the new thinner me. I would be standing on the deck looking across the lake and he'd be beside me, his hand wrapped around my naked waist.

Looking back I can see the folly of such dreams, but back then it seemed real enough to touch. Ryan had the ability to make fantasy seem real and black appear white. Once you were swept up in his dreams, there was no escaping.

BEFORE THE YEAR WAS OUT, the long hours and poor diet got to me. It started with an upset stomach that I blamed on the pizza we'd had the night before.

"I don't think it was the pizza," Ryan said. "I feel fine."

I'd skipped lunch, so regardless of what he said I knew it was the pizza. But the nauseous feeling hung on, and for rest of the week I couldn't look at food. By the time the weekend rolled around, I was convinced I had an ulcer.

"Uncle Harry had the same thing," I told Ryan. "It runs in our family."

I was pretty certain that by watching my diet I could get the ulcer under control, but the following Tuesday I was too sick to even go to work.

I stayed in bed until almost ten o'clock; then I forced myself to get up, pull on a pair of jeans and drive to the walk-in clinic.

"I've got a really bad ulcer and need to see a doctor," I told the receptionist.

My stomach was gurgling and the urge to throw up threatened to come back, but I still had to fill out the paperwork. Once I handed her back the clipboard, she ushered me into a small examination room and said Doctor Haussler would be with me shortly.

Doctor Haussler was a tall man with silver hair and wire-rimmed spectacles perched on the tip of his nose. He was still reading the paperwork I'd filled out when he walked into the room. He lifted his eyes, peered over the glasses and asked, "So, what makes you think you've got an ulcer?"

"It runs in my family," I explained. "Uncle Harry had the same problem."

He scrunched his forehead and gave me a strange look. "You seem rather young for ulcers. Have you gained or lost weight recently?"

"Lost," I answered. "And I've been sick to my stomach."

"What kind of sick? Nausea? Acid reflux?"

"Both. I haven't eaten anything, but I threw up again this morning."

"Is there a chance you might be pregnant?" he asked.

Ryan and I weren't married yet, so we'd been pretty careful most of the time. There might have been an occasional slip-up, but I doubted that was the problem. My stomach was flat as a pancake, and I was in what I considered to be my bikini shape.

"I don't think so," I said with a laugh. "Anyway, aren't pregnant women supposed to gain weight, not lose it?"

"It's not unusual for a woman to lose weight in the first trimester," he said. "Especially if she's had morning sickness."

"This hasn't been just in the morning."

"It can happen that way," he said. "Do you recall when you had your last period?"

I started thinking and couldn't remember. It had been a while, but I'd chalked it up to a hectic schedule and not eating.

"I'm not certain," I answered.

"Well, since a pregnancy test is the easiest, let's start there and rule that out before we go any further."

A FEW MINUTES LATER A nurse came into the room, drew a vial of blood, then left me sitting there. When Doctor Haussler came back he was smiling.

"Congratulations," he said. "You're having a baby." He hesitated then added, "I hope that's good news."

I nodded, even though at the moment the only thing I felt was shock. I left the clinic carrying a pamphlet with diagrams of what was happening inside my body and a list of obstetricians in the Burnsville area.

THE THOUGHT OF MOTHERHOOD GROWS on a woman faster than you might imagine possible. I'd started the day with what seemed to be an ulcer and now had a baby growing inside of me. According to Doctor Haussler it was eleven weeks old, no bigger than a fig, and yet had its own tiny little fingers and toes. That thought whizzed right by those dreams of having a big house with a pool and gave me a warm cuddly feeling.

I didn't call on any customers that day; instead I walked around town soaking up the warmth of summer. My senses seemed somehow sharper. I sniffed the air and caught the smell of potted geraniums, heard the rustle of birds hidden in the oak trees and even felt the breeze against my skin, warm with a whisper of dampness.

When I turned onto Broadmoor Boulevard I passed two women who appeared to be mother and daughter, the daughter pushing a baby in a stroller.

I peeked in at the tiny person with a pink sunbonnet tied beneath her chin. "She's adorable. How old is she?"

"Six months tomorrow," the mom answered.

I smiled and patted my almost non-existent stomach. "I just learned today that we're expecting a baby."

There is a universal joy in this type of news. It is something to be shared. The two strangers and I stood and talked for a good fifteen minutes, chatting about babies and the way they tie a family together. It wasn't until after they'd moved on that I realized I'd told two total strangers what I hadn't yet told Ryan.

TELLING RYAN WAS NOT SOMETHING to look forward to. I knew how he felt. None of his plans included a baby. Not one. They included a bigger house, a new car, a boat and even a vacation, but not a baby.

"That's a responsibility we don't need," he'd said and ticked off all the reasons. We were too young. We couldn't afford it.

Having a baby would put a stop to our savings and mean the end of all those dreams.

At the time I'd agreed with him. He'd painted such a beautiful picture of us swimming naked in the pool, making love on a boat, running off to some exotic vacation paradise, but all that was before. Back when having a baby was nothing more than an abstract thought. Now it was a reality.

Baby Versus Boat

The euphoric feeling I'd had walking around town slowly dissipated when I got home and started thinking of how to break the news to Ryan. He wasn't going to like the idea, but hopefully it would grow on him as it had on me. Trying to give myself every advantage, I showered, put on fresh makeup and dressed in an outfit he loved: a pale blue sundress the color of my eyes.

Ryan was later than usual, but when he got home he seemed in a great mood.

"Let's go out to dinner tonight," I suggested.

"Sounds good," he said. "Give me twenty minutes to grab a shower and have a beer." As he started upstairs he hollered down, "Nab a couple of beers and come join me."

Grabbing a single can from the fridge, I followed him up.

"Here you go," I said and handed him the beer.

"Nothing for you?"

I shook my head. "My stomach's still kind of upset."

"Then we won't go to dinner."

"Actually I'd like to go out," I said. "It'll give us a chance to talk."

"Talk?" he replied and gave me a look of apprehension. "About what?"

"Just things. Our life. Our plans for the future."

Ryan had a way of knowing when I had something on my mind, and he could usually tell whether it was good or bad.

"Oh, shit," he said and plopped down in the plaid club chair. "What now?"

"I went to the doctor today, and it's not an ulcer..." As I spoke I could hear the quiver in my voice.

Calm down, I thought. *This is Ryan. He loves you. Once he knows about the baby, he'll change his way of thinking.*

I tried to remember the phrases I'd put together, beautiful words to describe the joy of having a family, but seeing the steely set of Ryan's eyes took the words from my mind. I stuttered a few meaningless words then blurted, "I'm pregnant."

He looked like I'd smacked him in the head with a skillet. He sat there for a full minute then said, "You're kidding, right?"

"No, I'm not. I'm eleven weeks. The doctor said the baby is due mid-January."

If ever I needed someone to love me, it was at that moment. I prayed Ryan would walk over, wrap his arms around me and say something. Anything. I would have even welcomed him saying that he was glad I didn't have an ulcer.

But he didn't. He leaned forward, dropped his face into his hands and sat there sorrowfully shaking his head side to side. His silence was worse than a kick in the stomach. I waited several minutes then moved closer and stood directly in front of him.

"Say something."

"What can I say?" he replied. "You know how I feel. I'm not ready to be a father. Your timing is all wrong."

"My timing is wrong? Do you think I planned this?"

I wanted him to look up, see my face and understand how

much this meant to me, but instead he gave a lackadaisical one-shouldered shrug.

"Maybe, maybe not," he answered. "It doesn't matter."

"What do you mean it doesn't matter?"

"Either way, there's not going to be a baby."

I felt my eyes welling up. "There already is a baby! It's almost three months old! It has fingers and toes!"

He stood up from the chair and edged past me. "There's still time enough for you to do something, so I don't want to talk about it."

The thought of an abortion was like a snake slithering through my brain.

"I can't," I said. "I just can't."

With his back turned to me he said, "Well, you're going to have to do something because we can't afford a baby. Especially not now."

I followed behind him as he started down the stairs. "Why not now? Why is this different than any other time?"

He stopped and turned back. "Because I bought a boat today."

I gasped. "Bought a boat? How could you? We never talked about—"

"Yeah, Cheryl, we did," he cut in. "We talked about it a hundred times. What we never talked about was you having a baby." His words were edged with anger, his voice cold and unrelenting.

"Maybe we didn't talk about it in such precise terms," I replied, "but you must have realized that at some point—"

Before I finished the thought he said, "At some point maybe, but not now. Not when we're just getting started with our own life. We have plans. Places we want to go. Things we want to buy. Hauling a baby around is not—"

"We don't have to change our plans," I argued. "After the baby's born I'll go back to work. We can—"

"No!" he answered sharply. "I'm not going to raise a kid the way my mama raised me. I'm twenty-one years old and not ready to be a father. That's all there is to it." He hesitated a moment then tried to soften the thought by saying, "Sometime in the future, possibly, but not now."

By then I was already teary-eyed. "Is this about not wanting to marry me? Because if it is, we don't have to get married..."

He took my shoulders in a firm grip and looked directly into my face as he spoke.

"I do want to marry you," he said, "but not now and definitely not this way. Once we've had our fun and we've got the things we both want, then we can talk about having a baby."

"But what about this baby? What am I supposed to do about this baby?"

He took his hands from my shoulders, turned and picked up his beer.

"Do whatever you have to," he said and walked out of the room.

THAT EVENING WE WENT TO Gino's for dinner. We sat opposite one another and ate in silence. As I looked around the room and watched other couples talking and laughing together, I felt as lonely and forgotten as I did all those times I ate dinner with Mama. I sat there looking across the table at my baby's daddy and wishing I still had my Walkman.

OVER THE NEXT TWO WEEKS I talked to Ryan about the baby several times. I kept thinking maybe he'd change his mind, but he didn't. Each discussion only led to another argument. Countless times he reminded me that right from the start he'd made it clear he wasn't interested in having children.

"At least not right now," he'd say. He promised if I'd give up my thoughts of having this baby, we would get married and in time have a baby that we'd planned for.

As I've said, Ryan had a certain magic about him. He could tell you the most God-awful thing in the world and give it the sound of sweetness.

"I want you to have the best of everything," he'd say, "and that can't happen if you've got a baby to take care of."

According to Ryan, keeping this baby would mean we'd be stuck in our small house forever, never travel, never again make love and force him to get rid of the boat he'd always wanted. It seemed an awful lot of ramifications for one small baby, but after I'd listened to him long enough I began to think maybe he was right.

In the years ahead I would come to question whether I ever believed this or simply allowed myself to be manipulated into choosing between him and the baby.

I was nineteen years old and had no one else to turn to. Mama had pretty much disowned me, and Ryan was my only family. I was strong enough to work seventy hours a week, climb onto the roof and clean gutters, squat and paint baseboards and push a wheelbarrow many men couldn't have handled, but I wasn't strong enough to lose Ryan and have this baby all by myself.

Reluctantly, I made my decision.

FINDING A FAMILY

Other than Daddy, Ryan was the only man I'd ever loved, but after he pushed me into making a decision that went against everything I believed in I came within a hair's breadth of hating him. I say he pushed me, but he didn't really push; what he did was give me no alternative then leave me to make the painful decision.

Trust me when I tell you making the decision alone was far worse. I hated myself even more than I hated him. I hated myself for being a weak, spineless soul who didn't have courage enough to defend my baby.

The day I called the abortion clinic, I pretended to be asleep until I heard Ryan slam the door on his way out. Even then I waited until I heard the rumble of his truck leave the driveway and disappear down the block. Looking back maybe I waited because I thought by some miracle he'd come running back and say he'd changed his mind. Of course he didn't.

THE TELEPHONE RANG THREE TIMES; then a woman answered.

"Labara Clinic," she said. "This is Peggy. How may I help you?"

"I'd like to make an appointment for an abortion," I replied.

"Have you had your consultation?" she asked. Her voice was warm and friendly. I had no idea how old she was or what she looked like, but I pictured her as a grandmother with silver curls hugging her face.

"I've already been to the doctor, if that's what you mean."

"No, I'm referring to a consultation here at the clinic."

She said before I could arrange for a procedure, I would have to come in for a consultation. We were talking about an abortion, but she called it a procedure. I guess that was the politically correct term for killing a baby.

"We do this so you'll understand the process and be aware of what's going to happen," she explained.

"I know what happens," I replied angrily. "Three years ago I was part of an anti-abortion group that picketed the clinic in Back Bay."

She hesitated then asked the question I should have been asking myself.

"If that's how you feel about abortion, why on earth are you considering it?"

The tears I'd been holding back began to flow.

"It's not what I want," I said as I sobbed, "but I have no other choice." I explained that I was nineteen years old and not married.

Peggy was a stranger, a woman I'd probably see once and then never again; still I tried to give justification for this horrific deed I was about to do.

"My boyfriend doesn't want the baby," I said, "and I've got no way of caring for it by myself."

"Abortion isn't the only answer for someone in your situation," Peggy said. "Have you considered adoption?"

Until then I hadn't, but listening to Peggy talk about families who wanted babies and couldn't have them presented a new and slightly less painful option. I wouldn't be able to keep my baby, but at least I didn't have to kill it.

I never did meet Peggy and don't even know her last name, but I will forever be thankful for her wisdom. She sensed the agony in my heart and helped me wade through my misery to discover the truth. I wanted my baby to live.

That evening when Ryan asked if I had called the abortion clinic, I nodded. That was it. He had no questions, and I said nothing more.

CARRYING A BABY DOES SOMETHING strange to your heart; it opens it up and teaches you the meaning of unconditional love. I found myself thinking of the Disney movie *Dumbo*. In it a mother elephant attacks a crowd of circus goers because they make fun of little Dumbo's oversized ears.

At the time I thought it was just a cute cartoon, but suddenly I could see the significance of the story. It tells of a mother's overwhelming love for her baby. Dumbo's mother was protecting her child, and I was going to do the same. I pulled out the list of obstetricians Doctor Haussler had given me, picked one and made an appointment. By then I'd already promised myself I would start eating healthier and stop getting through the day with just a diet soda and candy bar.

All too soon the time would come when I'd have to give my baby to someone else, but for now it was mine to love and protect. I had another six months to be with this child, and I was determined to make the most of every single day.

TWO WEEKS LATER I CONTACTED the Family First Adoption Agency. Although I had come to accept that I couldn't keep the baby, I was going to try to give it a good home. A home where it was wanted and would be loved.

The agency was in a yellow brick building in the center of Dorchester. On the afternoon of my appointment, I parked in front of the building then resolutely pushed through the glass doors and stepped into the elevator.

Suite 308 was at the far end of the hall. I walked in and the receptionist, a girl who looked to be my age, glanced up and smiled.

"I'm here to see Melanie Dodd," I said. My words were thin and wobbly; they had the sound of a stranger's voice.

"Cheryl Ann Ferguson?" she asked.

"Yes," I answered.

She gave an acknowledging nod then came from behind the reception desk and ushered me down the hallway.

"Melanie is expecting you," she said and pointed toward the open door.

Melanie Dodd looked like a woman who once lived on the far end of Spruce Street. She was younger than I'd expected, with narrow shoulders and delicately boned hands. Her hair, a medium brown, was streaked with grey, but the thing you noticed was the emerald green color of her eyes.

She reached across the desk, shook my hand, then motioned for me to sit.

"I was just going to have my afternoon tea," she said. "Will you join me?"

"Um, I don't think—" I stuttered.

"Oh, you must," she urged. "It's dandelion tea, which is wonderful for renewing the spirit and relaxing the soul."

Before I could refuse she pulled two mugs from the credenza behind her desk, snapped on the electric water pot and began filling two infusers. We talked as she went about the task.

"I know this is an overwhelming decision," she said, "but rest assured, we will only do what is in your best interest. Nothing is carved in stone. If you change your mind and decide to keep the baby, you will have that prerogative."

"I won't," I said wistfully. Then I told her about Ryan and how he felt we had to get ourselves *established* before we could get married and start a family. I repeated all the reasons he'd given me: we were too young, we were just starting our careers, we had plans that didn't include a baby, we were building for the future.

When the tea was ready, Melanie handed me a mug and gave a non-judgmental smile.

"Let's talk about the type of family you'd like your child to have," she said.

We sat there for almost two hours talking about everything and nothing. Sitting across the desk from Melanie was like sitting at the lunch table with Nicole. It was a shared conversation that slid back and forth easily. When we finished the first cup of tea she brewed a second, then pushed aside a pile of papers and set a plate of Stella D'oro cookies on the desk.

She asked if I smoked, drank, did drugs or had a family history of addiction. I answered no to all the questions but mentioned Mama's love for coffee.

"Coffee has a lot of caffeine, but it's not considered an addiction," she said with a smile. "Personally I find tea a lot more relaxing. Especially dandelion tea."

I had to agree with her. Although I'd walked in with a knot of nervousness stuck in my chest, I felt better than I had in weeks. I can't say if it was the tea or the soothing sound of Melanie's voice, but I had begun to see a faint glow of something positive.

Before the afternoon was out, I'd described what I thought would be the perfect family for my baby. I wanted a Christian family, a stay-at-home mom with some college so she could help with homework and a dad who was patient and kind, a man who didn't travel for work and would be at home to spend evenings with his family.

"Tall," I said, "with brown hair and blue eyes..." As I continued I realized I was describing my daddy.

I had painted a picture of what I thought was the perfect family, but Melanie didn't laugh at all the small nuances I'd tucked in. She simply said to give her a few days, and she'd send over some binders for me to review. When we finished talking she came around the desk and gave me a warm hug.

"Don't worry," she said. "We're going to get this right."

I thanked her and started for the door; then at the last moment I turned back.

"That tea was so soothing," I said. "What kind was it?"

"Dandelion tea," she replied. "It comes from a charming little apothecary on the far side of Burnsville."

"That's fairly close to where we live. What's the name of the shop?"

"I don't know that it actually has a name," Melanie said, a twinkle in her eye. "It's just a little apothecary in the front of the Memory House Bed and Breakfast on Haber Street."

"I'll look for it and stop in," I said.

"If you do, please tell Ophelia Brown I send my love. She's such a darling."

MEMORY HOUSE

After my meeting with Melanie I took the long way home and drove past the apothecary. It was after six so my intent was to drive by, make note of where it was and then come back when I had more time.

I almost missed the sign because it was shadowed by a huge weeping willow. Behind a low-hanging branch I spotted the glint of what was once bright gold lettering and slowed the car.

Memory House Bed and Breakfast it read. There was no mention of the apothecary.

My curiosity got the better of me, and I turned into the driveway. As I came closer to the house I could see gold lettering on the front window: Apothecary. Inside the light was on, and a woman stood behind the counter.

Being I'm already here... I thought and pushed the gearshift into Park.

I STEPPED ONTO THE PORCH, rapped the brass knocker and called out, "Are you open?"

"Yes," a voice called back. "Come on in."

I twisted the knob and stepped into what looked like the

center hallway of someone's home. There was the scent of baby powder in the air.

"Over here," the voice said; then a silver-haired woman poked her head out of the door on the right-hand side. "Did you need something from the apothecary?"

I nodded then asked, "Are you Ophelia Browne?"

"I surely am," she answered.

"Melanie Dodd said to give you her love."

She smiled, and I could see a violet sparkle in her soft grey eyes.

"Are you a friend of Melanie's?" she asked.

Since this afternoon was the first time we'd met, I wasn't sure whether Melanie considered me a friend or not.

"Sort of," I answered. "I'm working with her."

"Well, then," Ophelia said with a laugh, "I bet you're here for dandelion tea."

"Yes, but how did you—"

"Melanie sends a lot of her prospective mothers here," she replied. "Dandelion tea has a relaxing effect that helps wannabe moms stay calm while they wait for Melanie to find them a baby."

Today I could have cried a dozen different times, but I'd held back the tears. This time it was impossible. I felt the heat of that first teardrop rolling down the side of my cheek.

"I'm not waiting for a baby," I stammered, "I'm giving mine away."

Ophelia Brown opened her arms and I fell into them, sobbing as if my heart would break. I told her things I hadn't told anyone else. Not Ryan. Not Mama. Not even Nicole. She listened as I poured out the story of how I was such a terrible mother and hadn't fought hard enough to keep my baby.

"Ryan and I lead such a selfish life," I said through my sobs. "Instead of loving this baby, he bought a boat!"

Ophelia gave a muffled chuckle. "But that's him, not you."

"I want those things too..." My words trailed off because I knew it wasn't the whole truth. Yes, I wanted those things, but if Ryan had agreed to keeping the baby I would have been deliriously happy with just having a family. The thought of swimming naked in a fancy pool paled in comparison to that of holding our baby to my breast.

Ophelia took my hand in hers and said, "Actually what you're doing is extremely unselfish. You're giving your baby a chance at a happy home and a good future."

"You really believe that's true?" I asked.

"I know it is. I've met a number of Melanie's clients and can tell you most of those women pray long and hard that one day she'll find a baby for them."

We talked for a long while, and even though I knew Ryan was going to be annoyed about dinner being so late I didn't rush out. Listening to Ophelia tell of the joy I would give someone else gave me a bittersweet sort of happiness.

When the sky turned dark and I turned to leave, Ophelia followed me to the door. She put her hand on my shoulder and said, "I know you can't see it now, Cheryl, but I can, and I promise you one day you'll have a house full of little ones. You'll be happier than you ever dreamed possible."

As I backed out of the driveway I saw Ophelia standing beneath the porch light, waving goodbye. *It's not goodbye*, I thought. Although this was the first time I'd met this strange and wonderful woman, I knew somehow it wouldn't be the last.

THAT NIGHT I TOLD RYAN I hadn't gone through with the abortion.

"I just can't do it," I said. "I'm going to have the baby and give it up for adoption—"

"If this is some kind of game you're playing, count me out. I've already told you, I can't deal with us having a baby right now."

"It's not—"

"Don't think I'm changing my mind. Maybe in the future, once we're established."

God, how I'd come to hate that word. *Established.* It reminded me of a business too big to care about its customers. A business with "Established in 1910" written under the name. I had no idea when the apothecary was established, but it didn't matter. The important thing was that Ophelia Browne cared about her customers.

"I've already spoken to an adoption agency," I said icily.

"Good," he said then gave a crooked half-smile, popped open another Budweiser and headed for the living room.

FIVE DAYS LATER MELANIE SENT over the binders she'd promised. There were four of them, each one representing a family who wanted a child. I set them aside, thinking after dinner Ryan and I would sit together and scour through the details.

Knowing how he felt about not keeping the baby, I thought he'd be anxious to help find a family. He came home in a bad mood because one of the workers failed to show up that day and he'd had to fill in behind the counter.

I waited until after dinner. By then he'd had two beers and was leaning back watching the Baltimore Orioles get killed by the Yankees. I plopped down on the sofa beside him.

"How's the game going?" I asked.

He groaned. "Terrible. Bernie Williams just hit another one out of the park."

"Melanie sent over four binders for us to look at—"

Without looking away from the television screen he asked, "Who's Melanie?"

"Melanie Dodd. The woman from the adoption agency."

"Oh."

"These books are profiles of families who'd like to adopt our baby."

We sat for five minutes with me watching him and him watching the TV.

"I thought maybe you'd like to go through them with me," I finally said.

He shook his head. "You do it; I wanna see this game."

"I could wait until later—"

"Nah, that's okay. You go ahead. Whatever you decide is fine by me."

I CAN'T SAY WHETHER RYAN saw the tears in my eyes, but if he did he never mentioned it. I picked up the stack of binders and carried them to the bedroom by myself.

That night I sat on the bed and went through every page of all four binders. I'm certain any one of those couples would have made wonderful parents, but something about Dean and LeAnn Stuart drew me in. Dean looked a bit like Daddy, younger and taller, but with that same crinkly smile. LeAnn was everything I wanted to be. She taught Sunday school to first grade kids, and the binder included a picture of her standing with a group of ten students. I noticed how LeAnn had her arm wrapped around a little blonde girl who was squished up against her leg. In her letter she wrote, "One of my greatest disappointments in life has been that I have been unable to bear a child."

After I had gone through all of the binders I turned back to the one about the Stuarts. Dean was a graduate of Duke. He worked with the Federal Reserve Bank of Richmond. LeAnn was an only child. She worked as a dental hygienist but planned to quit and be a stay-at-home mom if they were fortunate enough to find a baby to adopt. As I reread her biography, I noticed something else: she had studied at Bay River Junior College, the same school I'd planned on attending.

Their house was a mid-sized split level in Lawton, a town 74 miles south of Burnsville. There were photographs of the house and a floor plan showing the baby's room just steps from the master bedroom.

I reread each of their letters a third and then fourth time.

"It makes no difference whether the baby is a boy or girl," Dean wrote, "we would be equally happy with either one."

LeAnn promised that if they were fortunate enough to be given a baby, she would love and cherish the child for as long as she lived.

"Fortunate enough to be given a baby..." That phrase appeared in several different places, and I could almost hear LeAnn's voice speaking the words.

The next morning I called Melanie and said I'd like to meet the Stuarts.

THAT FRIDAY WE MET AT the Magic Mug, a coffee shop in downtown Wyattsville. Melanie and the Stuarts were already seated in a booth when I arrived.

Melanie spotted me and waved. As I walked toward the back, Dean slid from the booth and stood.

He reached out and took my hand in his. "Thank you so much for considering us. LeAnn and I are both thrilled at the prospect."

I couldn't help but notice how he was dressed: white shirt, midnight blue pinstriped suit and red tie. His shoes looked as if they'd just been polished. It's funny how a small thing like that becomes so important, but it does. Seeing him dressed that way made me feel he cared enough to be at his best. That was precisely the kind of daddy I wanted for my baby.

LeAnn was just as I imagined. Soft-spoken, with a smile you could feel as much as see.

Melanie did the introductions; then I slid in beside her. Dean sat next to LeAnn.

"We want to thank yo—"

"I'm glad you could—"

My words and LeAnn's overlapped one another. We both stopped, gave a nervous twitter and each deferred to the other.

I laughed. "You first."

She told me about the church they belonged to and how there were oodles of children in the neighborhood. I liked that LeAnn had blue eyes, the same as me. When she smiled I could tell by the lines at the corners of her eyes she was a person who smiled a lot.

Mama hardly ever smiled. She had dark brown eyes and a scowl that seemed to grow more solemn every year. I got my blue eyes from Daddy.

I sat there listening to LeAnn talk about what a good life my baby would have, but all the while I was wondering if the baby would have blue eyes like me.

Before lunch was over, I'd made my decision.

THE NINETEENTH WEEK

L ooking back I know that was the year my relationship with Ryan changed. We became two separate and very different people with only the plans we'd made tying us together. He was now district manager for nine stores, so he left the house early and got home late. When we were together we talked about jobs and ways to grow our bank account. We seldom made love and never spoke of the baby.

LeAnn Stuart was the person I'd call when I had an urge to talk about this tiny life growing inside of me. She was interested in every detail. She'd ask if I'd felt the baby move. Was my nausea getting better? Was there anything I needed? Twice she sent over a basket filled with fresh fruit, nuts, granola and jars of honey. And one Saturday she drove all the way over to Burnsville to bring me a book called *What to Expect When You're Expecting*. I noticed the spine of the book had already been cracked.

"Did you read this?" I asked.

She gave a sheepish nod. "I wanted to feel like I was a part of your pregnancy."

Since Ryan quite obviously didn't want to be, I welcomed the thought. I hugged her affectionately and invited her in. He was working that Saturday, so we sat with our cups of dandelion tea for almost an hour.

"I've begun walking three miles a day," I said.

"That's wonderful," she replied. "Walking is good for expectant mothers. It helps to avoid preeclampsia and…"

As she rattled on I knew she had not only read the book, she'd studied it.

THE MATERNAL FEELING THAT HAD settled in my heart superseded everything else. It fostered a spirit of love I wanted to share with the world. I began thinking about Mama and wondering if she'd had this same feeling when she was carrying me. In the years I'd been gone we'd spoken six, maybe seven times. I'd given her my telephone number, but she never called.

As much as I enjoyed talking with LeAnn, she hadn't gone through this and I wanted to talk with someone who had, someone who could understand the thrill of feeling a tiny baby twist and turn inside your stomach.

One afternoon I was driving home from Wyattsville I thought about Mama and decided to call her when I got home.

"It's been a long time since we last talked," I said, then told her about having the baby.

She groaned. "Lord God, Cheryl, Aren't you ever gonna get any sense?"

I didn't want to talk about the right or wrong of us not being married or the misery of knowing I would one day have to give this baby away. I only wanted to talk about what I was experiencing. There was dead silence on her end as I gushed over my feelings for the baby.

"I'm exercising and eating right because I love this little baby and want the best for it," I said. "Didn't you feel that way when you were carrying me, Mama?"

"Hardly," she replied. "You were a problem from day one. I was sick the entire time, and all I remember is nine months of puking my guts out."

No matter what I said, Mama came back with a negative retort. When I spoke about the joy of knowing the baby had grown ears and fingernails, she talked about the constant pain in her back. When I told her how I sang and talked to the baby, she claimed that was nothing but damn foolishness. Finally I told her I had to get going, and we said goodbye. The minute we hung up I scratched a line through Mama's number in our address book. It was a small act of rebellion but one she deserved.

I'd spent the first seventeen years of my life in that house and knew the number by heart. Sooner or later I would rewrite the number on a new line but not now. Not while I wanted to enjoy the sweetness of loving this baby.

THAT NIGHT I TOLD RYAN I'd called Mama.

He rolled his eyes and said nothing. This had become our way of life. We simply didn't talk about these things. Although by now the rise of my stomach was obvious, he never acknowledged it. During the months of pregnancy I had a swell of raw emotions I wanted to share, but Ryan was not willing to listen. To him this was simply a time to be tolerated. Another four months until we could go back to the life we'd been living. Another four months until we could pretend it never happened.

I WAS NINETEEN WEEKS WHEN Doctor Peters, my obstetrician, scheduled an ultrasound. Seeing a picture of the baby growing inside of you is kind of like witnessing a miracle, and I thought perhaps if Ryan saw it he'd better understand what I was feeling.

"Today I'll get to see whether we've created a boy or girl," I said. "You want to come with me?"

He didn't stop to think before he shook his head. "We're short a man in the Grant Street store. You can tell me tonight."

At that moment I can't say if I was angrier with him for not caring or myself for being foolish enough to think he would.

THAT DAY IS STILL VIVID in my mind. It was the third Thursday of September and cooler than usual. Dark clouds scuttled across the sky, and I could feel rain in the air. It hadn't yet started when I left the house. I had three customers to see that morning and my ultrasound appointment at two o'clock. If I finished up early I was planning to stop in Cooper's Appliances and talk to them about increasing their ad budget.

Shortly after eleven the rain began. It started with a light mist, but by the time I'd finished my third call it was coming down in torrents. I remember walking into the doctor's waiting room with my shoes squishing.

The rain slowed everything that day, so the sonographer was running behind. There was one other woman ahead of me, and in an obstetrician's office pregnant women tend to talk to each other.

"When are you due?" she asked.

"January fifteenth," I answered. For the moment I allowed myself to pretend I was like her, a woman carrying a baby that would forever be hers. I stuck out my hand and said, "Cheryl Ann Ferguson."

"Alicia Martin," she replied.

We chatted for about five minutes, and she confided in me that she was hoping for a boy.

"We're already got two girls," she said, "so a boy would be nice."

"I'd be happy with either," I said, echoing LeAnn's words.

"Actually I would be too," she replied. "As long as the baby's healthy."

Moments later her name was called, and for the next twenty minutes I sat there leafing through a *Parents* magazine. During that time I pictured my own baby and imagined it to be a girl.

Just as she came from the back office smiling, my name was called. As I walked toward the waiting nurse, I looked over and mouthed the words, "A boy?"

She gave a happy nod and disappeared out the door.

I CLIMBED ONTO THE TABLE and leaned back. After running around in the rain all morning, these few moments of doing nothing felt rather relaxing.

"I'm going to squirt a little bit of gel on you," the technician said; then a blob of warm jelly landed on my stomach.

That's how it was; he announced each thing as he went through the motions. At first he sat back, smoothly sliding the wand through the gel, moving from one spot to the next.

"It looks like you're having a girl," he said. Then he leaned forward and frowned at the monitor.

At first I thought that was the end of the ultrasound, but it wasn't. He squirted another glob of gel on my stomach and this time he moved the wand slower, sometimes less than a millimeter in one direction then back again in the other. Minutes ticked by, and I noticed how he watched the screen with ever increasing intensity.

Alicia had been in and out in twenty minutes. I glanced at the clock on his desk. I had been on the table for more than an hour.

"Is something wrong?" I asked.

"No, no," he replied nervously. "I just need to have Doctor Peters take a look at this." He left me on the table and scurried out of the room.

Moments later the doctor followed him back and waited as the technician slid the wand across my stomach. The two of them had that same worried frown as they eyed the image on the screen.

By then I was starting to worry. "What's wrong?"

"It may be nothing," Doctor Peters said, "but..."

The tone of his voice caused my heart to start banging against my chest.

"Just to be on the safe side," he said, "I'm going to refer you to a perinatologist. That's a maternal-fetal medicine specialist."

I gasped. "Oh, my God, what's wrong with my baby?"

"Right now there's nothing to worry about," he said, but it was too late. I'd already seen the look on his face.

I didn't call on any other customers that afternoon. I left the doctor's office, walked back to my car and sat there watching the rain splash against the window as I cried my heart out.

BABY GIRL

Fear of the unknown is the biggest, meanest and ugliest fear of all. The unknown leaves it up to your imagination to think of the absolute worst that can happen. You don't even consider there might be something between ideal and horrific; you just go straight to worrying about the horrific. By the time I arrived home I was already imagining the worst.

Thursday was Ryan's bowling night, and in an odd way I was glad to be alone. I sat in the lounge chair, pushed back and cradled my tummy with my right hand.

"Baby girl," I whispered, "I am so sorry. So very, very sorry."

I remained there for more than an hour, talking to my baby, holding her in my arms and making tiny circles with my fingers on spots I thought were the cap of her head and the heel of her foot.

Then it was eight o'clock, and I could wait no longer. The Stuarts knew I was scheduled for the ultrasound today, and I had promised to call and tell them the sex of their baby. I dialed their number, and LeAnn answered on the first ring.

I'd barely said hello when she asked, "What's wrong?"

"I don't know yet," I said, "but I think there might be something wrong with the baby."

Dean picked up the extension. "Cheryl?"

Once they were both on the line, I told them the baby was a girl then explained my experience with the ultrasound.

"I've been referred to a specialist but the earliest appointment I could get was Tuesday morning, so I won't know anything more until then."

I heard a sniffle on the other end of the line and knew it was LeAnn.

"Don't worry," I said. "If something is wrong with the baby, I'm not going to hold you to your commitment."

"This is our baby," LeAnn said firmly. "She's ours, and we want her regardless of what's wrong."

Dean echoed that sentiment.

We all cried that night. We tried to reassure one another that it could be something small, something not worthy of worry. That's what we told one another, but none of us believed it. The only thing I knew for certain was that I had indeed picked the right parents for my baby girl.

THEY SAY ADVERSITY DRAWS PEOPLE together, and I believe it's true. Right from the start I'd had a good relationship with Dean and LeAnn, but when this new threat showed itself they became my staunchest supporters. They gave me what Ryan did not: a shoulder to lean on, an ear to listen, a heart to care.

After four days of living in what can only be described as a hell of unknown fears, Tuesday morning finally arrived. This time I didn't go alone. I had people who cared about my baby and me.

Dean and LeAnn drove over from Lawton, which with morning traffic is a ninety-minute trip, and they picked me up shortly before nine. Doctor Greenberg's office was another forty-five minutes back toward Lawton. The round trip of coming to pick me up, driving back to the doctor's office, then bringing me home and returning home themselves entailed almost five hours of driving.

"I could have just driven over and met you," I told them.

"Nonsense," LeAnn said. "You shouldn't have to face something like this alone." As we climbed from the car and started into the doctor's office she took my hand in hers. "This is our baby, and whatever there is to face we'll deal with it together."

We barely had time to sit before we were called in to see Doctor Greenberg. Instead of an examination room, we were ushered into a conference room with a mahogany table and black leather chairs.

Doctor Greenberg sat on one side of the table with a spread of notes in front of him. We sat on the opposite side. After a few brief introductions, he opened the folder and said, "I've already studied the ultrasound report, and unfortunately it appears that the baby has gastroschisis."

"Gastro—"

Before I could ask the question, he pulled out a medical illustration and placed it in front of us.

"Gastroschisis is a birth defect that takes place early in the pregnancy. The baby's abdominal wall has a hole in it, and the intestines grow on the outside of the baby's body rather than on the inside." He pointed to the specifics of the illustration. "The hole is most often here, to the right of the baby's belly button."

I looked at the illustration and felt like the floor of the room was being pulled from beneath me.

"Why?" I asked, my voice no more than a whisper. "Did I do something to—"

Doctor Greenberg shook his head. "It's nothing you did. It's not a genetic or chromosomal syndrome, it's a birth defect. It happens maybe once in every ten thousand births; more with teenaged mothers, but still a one in ten thousand shot."

"Can we do something to fix it?" Dean asked.

"Yes, there is a corrective procedure," Doctor Greenberg said, "but we can't do it as a fetal surgery; we'll have to wait until after the baby is born."

"Will she be okay then?" I asked.

Doctor Greenberg fingered his chin thoughtfully. "Maybe, maybe not. There's a ten percent mortality rate for babies born with gastroschisis. And even if the surgery is successful, there's still the possibility she'll have problems with digestion and the absorption of nutrients."

For a brief moment I let my mind linger on the thought of that unfortunate ten percent. Then I asked, "Is there something I can do to better her odds?"

"Take care of yourself. Don't get overtired or stressed. Eat healthy. I've seen this before, and I know what we're dealing with here. So don't worry, we'll be well prepared."

He spoke at length about what we could expect going forward. The likelihood was that they would deliver the baby sometime between 35 and 38 weeks rather than allowing me to go the full 40. And the probability was it would be a Cesarean delivery.

"Why would you take the baby early?" LeAnn asked.

"So we can schedule the date and have a pediatric team standing by," he said. "The baby will go straight from the delivery room into surgery."

He began to gather up his papers, then turned to me and said, "Oh, and I want to see you in here every two weeks."

Suddenly I had become a high-risk pregnancy that warranted a specialist. From here on in he would monitor the baby's progress, and we would make each decision as we went along. This was only the first step in what would be a long and rocky road.

THAT NIGHT I PRAYED HARDER than I had since I'd asked God not to take Daddy.

"Please," I begged, "let Doctor Greenberg be mistaken. Let my baby girl be born with every tiny little part in just the right place."

I knew the baby was not destined to be mine, but I loved her all the same. It was a strange feeling; I was her mother, but only for a short while. Another four months. Maybe less.

Even if it was only for that little bit of time, I wanted her to know I loved her. I wanted her to feel my arms around her and hear my voice. I had no right to name her, but in the strange way that only a mother can understand I did. I knew if I gave her a real name I would never be able to let her go, so I called her Baby Girl.

I prayed with her, sang to her and held her in my arms as together we began our sad and treacherous journey.

Too Soon

In the weeks that followed the appointment with Doctor Greenberg, my lifestyle changed dramatically. It started with a cut back in the number of hours I worked and carried over into everything else. For the first time in years I began making room in my day for good things: relaxation, visiting with friends and meals on a regular schedule.

In the morning when I felt fresh and rested I'd drive around, visit a few customers, then return home and have lunch at our old oak table. I'd fix a fresh green salad and bowl of soup, then eat leisurely as I browsed through magazines like *Good Housekeeping* and *Ladies Home Journal*.

In the afternoon, I worked from home. Instead of traveling from place to place, I called customers on the telephone. I sat in the big lounge chair with a few folders and a notepad in my lap, reclined the back and conducted business as easily as I did in face-to-face meetings. If I finished my calls early, I'd drive over to the apothecary and stay for a cup of dandelion tea.

Ophelia knew Baby Girl was scheduled for adoption, and on days when I needed to pour my heart out she was there to listen. No matter how much sorrow I spilled out, she had a way of making me feel better. Not patronizing, just listening and caring.

There was nothing I didn't share with Ophelia, and she in turn shared the stories of her life with me. As we sat at the kitchen table with honeyed cups of tea, she spoke of Edward, the husband she'd lost some thirty years earlier, and I talked of Ryan, not as we were a year ago but as we were now.

Her stories were filled with thoughts of love and longing. I can't say exactly what mine were filled with. Anger, maybe, or perhaps disappointment.

"He pretends this baby doesn't exist," I explained. "If he really loves me, he'd take more of an interest."

Ophelia reached across the table and placed her hand on my arm. "I doubt this is about you. More likely it's about Ryan himself."

"Ryan? But why—"

"I imagine he feels guilty about making you give up the baby."

"Him, guilty?" I scoffed. "I doubt—"

"You never know what's inside a person's head," she said. "Indifference is often a cover for guilt."

I thought about Ophelia's words for a long time and decided there could be a grain of truth to them. So Ryan and I continued, with each day folding into the next and nothing changing. He never mentioned the baby, and I stopped expecting him to care. Maybe we both thought that once she was no longer a part of our life, we'd go back to the way we were.

Unfortunately such a thought is never realistic. Once a link is broken, the chain no longer has strength. You can try to glue the pieces together and sometimes it holds for a while, but sooner or later it falls apart again.

There were good days and bad days. On a good day I lived in the moment, wrapping my arms around Baby Girl, talking to her and lovingly running my fingers across the swell of my stomach. When I felt her move I could tell which spot was a foot and which was the crown of her head. On afternoons when she seemed restless I sang to her and we danced. With my stomach cradled in my hands I waltzed across the room to the tune of *I Will Always Love You*. Over and over again I played that song, praying someday it would strike a familiar chord in her ear and she'd remember.

TWICE A MONTH I HAD an appointment with Doctor Greenberg, and LeAnn almost always came with me. Together we'd look at the sonogram and see the baby getting bigger and stronger, the mass of her intestines still on the outside of that tiny body and growing ever more obvious. The good thing was that the doctor had determined a vaginal birth would be better, barring any complications.

IN EARLY DECEMBER THE PAINS in my lower abdomen began. Fearful I might be going into pre-term labor, Doctor Greenberg put me on strict bed rest.

"You mean no driving?" I asked.

He wrinkled his brow and gave me a frown that resembled Mama's. "Bed rest means total bed rest! You're not to get out of bed for anything other than to use the toilet or take a shower. A very quick shower!"

"But..."

"There are no buts," he said. "Start jumping in and out of bed, and you're liable to go into labor. It's too early. The baby's not strong enough yet. We've got to keep you stable until we're ready with a pediatric team on hand and know she's strong enough to handle the surgery."

DOCTOR GREENBERG'S WORDS LEFT NOTHING to doubt. All of a sudden I was responsible for more than just Baby Girl's care and nourishment. I was responsible for her life. The thought scared me to death, and I think LeAnn was almost as frightened as I was.

In all the years we'd been together, this was the most challenging situation Ryan and I had ever faced. Bed rest might sound simple, but for us it wasn't. I had to take a leave of absence, so without my salary Ryan worked overtime and Saturdays to pay for the house, the boat and the investment property he was fixing up. It was up to our friends and neighbors to come and care for me.

Each morning he brought me breakfast before he left and made certain the telephone was on the table beside the bed.

"If you need anything call me," he'd say, then kiss me goodbye and be gone until seven or eight o'clock that evening.

Thank God for Emma Murphy, our next-door neighbor. She never left me alone for more than an hour or two. All day long she was in and out.

"Do you want a drink of water?" she'd ask. "Or a cup of tea?" When she wasn't offering something to drink, she tried to feed me or place a heating pad over my constantly cold feet.

All I could do was sit in bed and worry.

Emma would wait until she looked out the window and saw a car in our driveway; then she'd know I had company and dash off to do her own errands.

Most every day someone was there. Monday through Friday Nicole came straight from work and stayed until Ryan got home. LeAnn came four or five times a week, and more often than not she brought the banana split I craved. When LeAnn didn't come, she called.

"Do you need anything?" she'd ask. Lawton was more than an hour's drive away, but she never once hesitated about coming to check on me or bring something I needed.

Ophelia, bless her heart, came every day. She brought small gifts: homemade soup with fresh vegetables, zucchini bread, teas of a dozen different flavors, a book of poetry, scented candles and my favorite: a small dish of potpourri with the scent of baby powder.

"It won't always smell like baby powder," she warned. "Once you've moved on to thinking of other things, that fragrance will be gone."

I remember how I laughed and laughed at such a thought.

JANUARY 4, 1998

The alarm rang at 5AM. I reached over, turned it off and then gave Ryan's shoulder a gentle shake.

"We'd better get started," I said.

He gave a weary nod, brushed the sleep from his eyes, then came around to my side of the bed and helped me to stand. My legs were wobbly from all those weeks of being in bed.

This was going to be Baby Girl's birthday.

As Ryan showered and dressed, I washed my face and pulled on a pair of gray sweatpants with an oversized sweatshirt. By six o'clock we were on our way out the door.

"Don't forget my bag," I said.

Ryan helped me into the car then ran back inside and grabbed the tote bag I'd left sitting in the hall. There were no baby clothes in it, just an outfit I could wear home, two nightgowns, a jar of face cream, a hairbrush and a pale pink lip-gloss.

He plopped it into the back seat then climbed into the driver's seat.

"Are you ready?" he asked.

I nodded. Physically I was ready, but emotionally I was tied down by the feelings tugging at my heart. There was the joy of having kept Baby Girl safe all these months, the fear of knowing that before the day was out she'd be under a surgeon's knife and the brokenhearted realization that our time together was rapidly coming to an end.

When we arrived at the Angel of Mercy Hospital, LeAnn and Dean were waiting in the lobby. Leaning heavily on Ryan's arm, I looked over and gave them a smile.

LeAnn came to my side and kissed my cheek. "I've been praying for you and the baby all night," she whispered. She squeezed my hand then stepped back.

All of the paperwork had been done days earlier. They were ready and waiting. The nurse at the admissions desk snapped a plastic band on my wrist and the aide wheeled me off.

Much to my surprise, Ryan came along. He walked beside the wheelchair and when we moved into the elevator, he reached down and took my hand in his. He remained by my side as the nurse helped me into bed and inserted the IV of oxytocin that would induce labor.

It was late in the day before I actually began labor, but once it started everything seemed to happen at warp speed. Ryan was still sitting beside me, and I asked him to get the nurse.

"The baby's coming."

"Hopefully soon," he replied.

"No!" I shouted. "I mean right now!"

In the blink of an eye I was in the delivery room. Ryan was still with me. He held my hand and whispered, "Hang in there, honey, it'll all be over soon."

The truth was there, hidden behind his words of encouragement perhaps, but still there. For Ryan this was the bridge to be crossed. This was the step that would take us back to the life we'd lived before. Before there was a baby to think about.

Moments after Baby Girl was born she was scooped up, washed and wrapped in a warm saline-soaked cloth to cover her exposed intestines. The nurse handed her to me. I held her in my arms for less than a minute; then she was gone.

It felt as if I'd lost an arm or leg. For almost nine months, she'd been part of me. She ate what I ate, she drank what I drank, she'd been mine to love. And now I had only the emptiness she left behind. A thousand times I'd reminded myself of all the reasons why giving the baby up was better for her, but I'd turned a blind eye to the heartache it would cause me—until now. A warm flow of tears rolled down the side of my face.

With the tip of his fingers Ryan brushed them back, then leaned over and kissed me.

"Don't cry, sweetheart," he said. "It's all over now."

I turned my face to the wall without answering, but I knew it wasn't over. The weight of her loss was only beginning to settle in my heart.

BABY GIRL WENT FROM MY arms straight to the pediatric operating room. Before I was back in my bed, she was in surgery.

I knew that's how it would be, but knowing didn't make it any easier. Surgery was difficult enough for an adult, so I couldn't imagine how a tiny little thing like her could withstand such an ordeal. All these months I had fed her, cared for her and kept her safe. Now there was nothing more I could do. That thought broke my heart.

A dozen different times Ryan asked how I was doing, but he never once asked about that poor little baby and I hated him for it.

During the five hours Baby Girl was in the operating room, the nurses darted in and out of my room with updates. Looking back on that time it's somewhat of a blur, but I remember a nurse with hair the color of a firecracker. She was the one who came into my room and said Baby Girl was out of surgery and doing well.

"She's a real little trooper," the firecracker said. "A lot like you."

I liked the thought that Baby Girl was like me and I wanted to ask why, but before I could the firecracker was gone from the room.

Once I knew my sweet baby had made it through the operation, I closed my eyes and let myself sleep. When I opened them again Ryan was gone.

THE NEXT MORNING A MAN with dark hair and a graying beard poked his head into my room.

"Got a minute?" he said and strolled in without waiting for an answer.

"I'm Doctor Arnold," he said and handed me a card that read, "Frank S. Arnold, M.D., Psychiatry."

"How are you feeling?" he asked.

"Okay, I guess." I asked why he was here.

"Just checking up on you," he said. He gave me an easy smile and continued. "I understand your baby is being given up for adoption. Are you okay with that?"

"Yes." I nodded. Actually I wasn't okay with it. I was miserable, but I had no alternative. Ryan had forced me to choose between him and the baby.

"Are you sure?" he asked.

Again I nodded. This was all part of the system. A system that didn't actually care if your heart was breaking but needed to ask these questions before it could move ahead.

We chatted for another few minutes. Then Doctor Arnold said for me to call if I needed to talk and he left. As I listened to his footsteps disappear down the hallway, I realized that what

Ophelia said was true. This was the most unselfish thing I could ever do. I chose Baby Girl's happiness over my own.

RYAN CALLED THAT EVENING, BUT he didn't come back to the hospital until the next morning when I was due to be released. I was dressed and sitting in a chair when he arrived.

"You look great, babe," he said and flashed the grin I'd fallen in love with.

"Appearances can be deceiving," I replied solemnly.

He gave a strange little laugh. "What you need is to get back to having fun again. And I know just the thing..."

He said he had tickets to the boat show that afternoon. Afterward we'd meet his buddies and go for pizza.

I didn't feel like seeing Ryan, never mind his loud-mouthed buddies. My heart was heavy, my breasts were starting to dry up and hurt like hell, plus I was wrapped in a longing for Baby Girl that was as dark as a shroud. All these angry thoughts were churning through my heart, and yet I didn't say a word about them. It was almost as if I could hear Mama's sarcastic voice saying, "You've made your bed, now lie in it!"

As we started toward the elevator, I asked Ryan if he'd been to the nursery to see the baby.

"Unh-uh," he said and shook his head. "It's better this way."

"But don't you want—"

He turned away before I could finish my question.

THERE ARE THINGS IN LIFE you never forgive. You say you've forgotten about it, that what's done is done and there's no use crying over spilled milk. You even lie to yourself and say all is forgiven, but some wounds are too deep to ever heal. I know that if I live to be a hundred, I will still remember the hurt I felt that day when we left the hospital.

We did go to the boat show. Ryan walked through the exhibits oohing and aahing over things he hoped to own one day. I trailed behind him with hatred in my heart and sorrow weighing me down like a sack of stones. Throughout the entire day neither Ryan nor either of his friends mentioned the baby or even the fact that I'd just given birth. It was as if we'd simply stepped back in time and picked up exactly where we left off.

LETTING GO

They named her Morgan. LeAnn said it was a family name on her grandmother's side. Baby Girl was going to be an integral part of their family. She'd have a grandmother she was named after and two parents who loved her. That was what I wanted. It was the choice I'd made. But letting go was like ripping away an adhesive patch stuck to my heart.

There is a state law that says if a baby is to be adopted, for the six weeks following birth the baby cannot live with either the birth mother or the adoptive family. This is the final fail-safe period. The time when either party can change their mind. In most cases the baby goes to a foster home, to a family who knows they have her for only this short window of time, a family who knows not to become attached.

In Baby Girl's case it was different. She remained in the hospital. She still had two smaller surgeries to go through before the hole in her abdomen would be fixed and she would be strong enough to go home.

She couldn't live with me, but I could visit her in the nursery and I did. Every day. LeAnn did also. We no longer came together, but our paths crossed often. When we were both there at the same time, LeAnn stepped back and allowed me to be the one who held Morgan.

Just as I will never forget Ryan's actions on the day I left the hospital, I will also never forget LeAnn's small acts of generosity and kindness.

Throughout those six weeks I came to the hospital every day. I sat in the nursery rocking chair and held Morgan in my arms. Every day I dabbed on a bit of the gardenia perfume I'd used throughout my pregnancy, hoping to implant a memory that would one day come to her mind.

Someday when she's older, she'll catch a whiff of gardenia and remember the mama who loved her.

At times when LeAnn wasn't in the room, I would whisper "Baby Girl" and hold her to my chest. I wanted her to know I was still here, that I had not turned my back or forgotten our time together. Physically I was giving Baby Girl to another family, but in my mind and heart she was and always would be my daughter.

ON THE DAY THE SIX-WEEK period ended I had to appear in court, stand before a judge and swear that I, of my own free will, was giving up any and all rights I would ever have to Baby Girl.

"Would you come with me?" I asked Ryan.

"Do I have to be there?" he said.

Legally he didn't have to; morally I hoped he would want to.

"Not really," I said. "But I thought maybe…"

"I've got a killer day ahead of me," he said. "How about if I just meet you for lunch afterward?"

"Don't bother," I said and shook my head. "I've got a busy afternoon."

I turned and walked out the door without another word.

On the drive to the courthouse I fought back the tears and bit down on my lip so fiercely the taste of blood settled in my mouth.

You can do this, I told myself and mechanically moved one foot in front of the other as I walked up the steps and into the courtroom.

The judge rattled off the details of Baby Girl's adoption then asked if I understood that I was forever giving up all rights to this child. I answered yes, signed the papers and in a few brief seconds she was no longer mine. I could no longer hold her in my arms or whisper my words in her ear.

She was forever, permanently and irrevocably, gone from my life, but I knew even then she would never be gone from my heart.

I LIED WHEN I TOLD Ryan I had a busy afternoon. I walked out of the courtroom facing nothing but an empty span of hours, emptiness that I knew would be filled with tears and the heartache of being alone. Yes, I could have stopped in to see some of my favorite customers, perhaps taken a client to lunch. I could have called Nicole or gone shopping and browsed through the department store, but I did none of these things.

I got in my car and drove straight to Memory House. Ophelia Browne was the one person who understood the impact of loss; with her I could speak the truth of my feelings. That strange little apothecary with its herbal teas and magical potions was the only place I could find solace and if ever I needed it, it was now.

I PARKED THE CAR IN the driveway, walked to the porch and clanged the cowbell. Without waiting for an answer I pushed the door open and walked in. Ophelia took one look at my face, climbed down from the step stool she was standing on and came to me.

"This was the day, wasn't it?" she said and wrapped her arms around me.

I could no longer hold back the tears. I leaned into her shoulder and let go of all the things I'd been holding back. At the moment I felt like the loneliest woman in the world. I'd given up my baby for Ryan, and now his love seemed like a thin veil of pretense.

That afternoon Ophelia flipped the sign on the door to "Closed" and led me back to her kitchen where we sat across from one another at an old oak table.

"Maybe I should have explained my feelings," I said. "Perhaps if I told Ryan how much I needed him to be with me, he would have come."

She gave an understanding nod and took my hand in hers. "It's not possible to know what another person will do. You can't force someone to care about the things you care about; all you can do is trust that if he really loves you, he'll find a way to help you move beyond this sorrow. Maybe not today, maybe not even tomorrow, but sometime in the foreseeable future."

"What if he doesn't?" I asked.

"Then maybe he wasn't the person you were meant to love."

"That's crazy," I said. "Of course Ryan is the person I'm supposed to love. I've loved him since the day I first saw him."

She gave a knowing smile. "That's not love. That's infatuation."

"It might have started with infatuation, but it's grown into love."

"For you maybe, but can you say the same about him?"

I thought about that for a while and wasn't sure of the answer.

"Love is like a flower," Ophelia said. "To keep it growing

you've got to nourish it and care for it. If you push it to the back of the kitchen windowsill and stop watering it, it dies."

As I listened to her words I thought about my relationship with Ryan. Perhaps I had pushed him to the corner windowsill. I was angry and resentful, yet I'd kept all those feelings to myself. Nothing would change the fact that Baby Girl was gone, so maybe it was time to stop blaming Ryan for what happened and let myself go back to loving him.

When I left Memory House that evening, Ophelia gave me a tin of tea made with lavender and damiana. It was a mix that supposedly brought about happiness and encouraged passion in a floundering romance.

A Time Of Renewal

Looking back on the past six months, I could see Ryan wasn't the only one at fault. Along with the baby I'd carried a huge chip on my shoulder, and all the while I'd been daring him to knock it off. He hadn't even tried, so in my mind that was proof enough he loved me.

That night I made his favorite chicken noodle casserole, and after dinner I sat beside him on the sofa and watched a basketball game. I can't tell you who won or even which teams played, but I remember that halfway through the game Ryan leaned his thigh against mine and wrapped his arm around my shoulder.

That weekend he asked if I'd like to take a drive to the marina.

"I want to check on the boat, and maybe we could have dinner at the clubhouse," he said.

For the past year the boat had been a bone of contention between us. I'd seen it as the reason he didn't want the baby, and he'd seen it as a measure of our success. Whenever he'd mentioned it, I'd given him a scowl and a snide comment. He'd gone to the boat numerous times the previous summer but either by himself or with one of his friends.

Those same scissor-sharp words were right there on the tip of my tongue, but this time I stopped myself from saying them.

"Okay," I replied, "that sounds nice."

Before I could rethink what I'd said I busied myself in the kitchen, and Ryan headed for the garage whistling a happy tune.

WE HAD FUN THAT WEEKEND, and I think for the first time in almost a year I found myself laughing. Not just pretending to laugh but actually chuckling. Ryan was like he was that first summer when he took me to the Fourth of July fireworks—playful and even a bit naughty.

We had dinner at the little tavern in town and sat in a back booth where it was dark. Instead of sitting across from one another, he slid in beside me and playfully traced his fingers along the inside of my thigh. We drank wine and danced. It felt good to have him pressing his body against mine, to feel the heat of his breath on my neck and hear him whispering naughty suggestions in my ear.

That night we didn't go back to the house. We slept on the boat and made love for the first time in ages. We weren't where we once were, but perhaps we were moving toward it.

In many ways that was a really good summer. Our careers were both going great, and in early August Ryan found a second investment property that he was able to buy for next to nothing.

"It needs a bit of work," he said, "but what we get for rent will cover the mortgage with a few hundred to spare."

For two weeks we spent nights and weekends fixing up the place. Nothing major, just some cabinets from Home Depot, a coat of paint, a few flowers in the yard. Then, just as Ryan had predicted, it rented for almost twice what the mortgage cost.

That weekend we celebrated. We filled the cooler with food and two bottles of champagne and headed for the boat. That night instead of returning to our slip, we motored out to the deep waters of the Chickahominy River and dropped anchor. We made love, not in the cabin where we usually did, but outside on the open deck with the stars above us and the cool night air brushing across our skin.

Afterward Ryan raised himself up on one elbow and leaned over me.

"I think it's time," he said.

"Time?" I echoed. "For what?"

"It's time we got married."

"Really?"

"Yes, really," he said and brought his mouth down against mine.

LESS THAN A MONTH LATER we were married and on our way to Ocean City for a five-day honeymoon. We stayed at the Grand Hotel on Baltimore Avenue in a room with a balcony overlooking the ocean. We slept late every morning then ordered breakfast from room service. The coffee was served with thick cream on the side and biscuits so light it's a wonder they didn't float away.

Ryan and I had good times and bad times; our honeymoon was one of the really good times. As we stretched out beneath the warm sun or strolled hand in hand along the boardwalk, I felt safe and sure of our future.

THE CHRISTMAS AFTER WE WERE married, Ryan gave me a gift that made me happier than anything I could have ever wished for. It was Christmas Eve, and we had almost finished unwrapping presents.

"Oh, I do have one more gift for you," he said and handed me a small flat box wrapped differently than the others. "I think this might be what you've been wishing for." Before I opened it, he wanted me to try and guess what it was.

I took the box in my hands, felt the feathery weight of it and then gave it a gentle shake. No sound.

"A sexy nightie?"

He shook his head and gave a mischievous grin. "Something better."

"Better?" I felt the weight of the box again and gave a few more guesses. "A scarf? Socks? Panties?"

He laughed. "Not even close." Then told me to go ahead and open the box.

I anxiously tore the paper off and lifted the lid. It was a tiny white baby sweater and pinned to it was a note that said, "It's time."

It took all of about ten seconds for the thought to sink in. I looked at Ryan and said, "Does this mean—"

He nodded happily. "It's time for us to start our family."

I gave a squeal of joy that could be heard for three blocks in any direction and leaped across the pile of presents into his arms.

That Christmas was the happiest ever. Up until then we were like two separate cinder blocks sitting side by side. A baby was the mortar that would hold us together forever.

A NEW YEAR

Thoughts of another baby made it almost impossible to sleep. In ten days Morgan would celebrate her first birthday, and although Ryan and I never spoke of her she was seldom out of my mind. By this time next year she would probably have a sister or brother. I closed my eyes and tried to picture them getting to know one another, meeting for play dates, running around the playground while LeAnn and I sat on the park bench and chatted happily.

Try as I may, I couldn't bring that picture to mind. It was a fantasy beyond imagination. Over the course of the past year I had spoken to LeAnn twice, and while she was pleasant enough there was never a mention of my coming to see Baby Girl.

Both times I'd called on the pretext of asking about Morgan's health.

"Have there been any problems with her digestive system?" I asked.

LeAnn said there had been a few, but they were working through them.

I dredged up a few more questions about the surgeries but didn't ask the things I really wanted to know. I didn't ask if her eyes had turned the blue of mine, or she'd learned to sit or crawl, if she had gotten her first tooth or if she was learning to say Mama.

"If she ever needs me—" I'd said.

"Don't worry," LeAnn replied. "We'll be sure to call."

Of course I never heard from her. That's how these things work. When the judge asked if I knew I was giving up any and all claims to Baby Girl, that's exactly what he meant. I no longer had the right to even speak to her.

The only thing I hadn't given up were the memories of holding her in my arms. They were mine to keep. For a lifetime.

THAT NIGHT IT WAS NEAR dawn when I finally fell asleep, but for the first time in more than a year I was deep down happy. I would never have Baby Girl, but Ryan and I would have a child of our own. A child Ryan wanted. A baby with a name, one who would fill the empty spot in my heart.

The early months of that year seemed gloriously happy. We were together and working toward the same goal. In February Ryan bought a third investment property, another house that needed work. Once it was fixed up and rented, we again celebrated. It was too cold to go out on the boat, so we went to dinner then came home and made love.

Afterward we lay in bed, my head on his shoulder and my leg looped across his.

"With a few more investment properties," he said, "we won't be so dependent on your income. Maybe you can cut back and work from home after the baby is born."

I smiled at the thought, but the truth was I liked my job.

"Don't worry," I said. "I can handle the baby and my job." It seemed everything was now going our way, so I was brimming over with exuberant confidence.

Ryan laughed. "That's my girl."

I remember how we called it "the baby" and spoke as if it were a sure thing, something already ordered and just waiting to be shipped.

THAT WINTER WE MADE LOVE often. For the first three months it was spontaneous and exciting, but when March turned into April and I still wasn't pregnant I began to worry. I started planning our lovemaking sessions. I counted the days between one period and the next and took my temperature four times a day, trying to zero in on the exact moment of ovulation.

Twice I called Ryan at work and asked him to come home so we could have sex.

"I'm ovulating," I said.

The first time I asked he came home, but I guess his mind was still back at work because he couldn't do it. It was the only time something like this had happened, and he was none too happy about it.

"This is supposed to be fun," he said, "but you're making it feel like work."

We didn't make love for the remainder of that week. When we went to bed he turned on his side with his back to me. I knew he was aggravated with me and with himself, so on Saturday morning I packed a picnic basket and suggested we go to the boat.

Ryan enjoyed a lot of things: fixing up old houses and turning them into an investment, bowling with his buddies, car shows, action-packed movies and a dozen other things, but most of all he enjoyed being on the boat. We spent the afternoon on the river, jumping off the boat, floating in the tube then climbing back up the ladder so chilled our teeth chattered. That evening we fired up the portable hibachi, grilled hamburgers on the back deck and washed them down with cold beer. It was near midnight when we finally climbed into the bunk and fell asleep.

On Sunday morning we made love, and everything was back to normal.

THE SECOND TIME I CALLED and asked him to come home so we could work on making a baby, he refused.

"I'm busy, Cheryl," he said. "It can wait."

Obviously just thinking about it was a turn-off for him, because he waited five days and by then I was well past my time of ovulation. When he finally did want to make love, I turned on my side and ignored the way he was kissing my shoulder and sliding his hand along the curve of my hip.

LOVE IS A FUNNY THING; it can be strong enough to overcome the greatest obstacle imaginable or so fragile that it breaks apart from a few harsh words or careless slights.

After six months of trying to conceive and failing miserably, I began to believe this was God's punishment for not appreciating the first baby He'd given me. I went back to thinking of Baby Girl and missed her more than ever. Some days I'd be driving and have to pull to the side of the road to wipe the tears from my eyes because of thoughts that I'd never have another child.

Whenever I mentioned this to Ryan, he'd roll his eyes as if he couldn't bear the thought of discussing it yet again. In my mind I felt we'd never discussed it—not openly and honestly. There had been a few digs and nasty innuendos but never once a heartfelt conversation.

To his way of thinking it was just the opposite. He saw it as a subject that reared its ugly head more frequently than he could tolerate. Just the mention of Baby Girl or the difficulty I was having in getting pregnant started an argument.

"This is all your fault!" I'd scream. "If you hadn't made me give up my baby..."

It was an open-ended dispute that went nowhere. More than once Ryan stormed out saying I was impossible to live with.

THAT SUMMER OUR RELATIONSHIP SEESAWED back and forth. We'd be good for a week or two, then I'd get my period and go back to being resentful again.

We didn't just suddenly stop making love, but the instances grew further and further apart. I'd have a headache. He'd be exhausted. It stopped being a pleasure and slowly turned into a symbol of failure. Our failure to make another baby.

ONCE A RELATIONSHIP IS BROKEN, sometimes there is no way to fix it. For a while we both tried, but in time I guess we gave up trying. Instead of whispering naughty things in my ear, Ryan talked about replacing the screen door on one of the houses or buying a secondhand washer for another one.

The black lace nightie he'd bought me on our honeymoon was now stashed in the bottom drawer. After work I'd slip into a comfy pair of pajamas and curl up with a book. Little by little, piece by pitiful piece, the magic we once had slipped away.

Several nights a week Ryan had dinner out, supposedly staff meetings with the employees from one store or another. With him not home, I'd meet Nicole and we'd go out for a drink. Towards the end of September, he started going to the boat alone. The first time he said it was because he needed to work on the engine.

"Do you need help?" I asked.

He shook his head. "Nah. This is stuff I've got to do myself; there's no sense in you just hanging around."

That Friday evening he tossed a few things in a gym bag and took off. I didn't see him again until late Sunday.

The next weekend it was the same thing. Even after the weather turned cold, he found reasons to go to the marina once or twice a month.

TWO WEEKS BEFORE THANKSGIVING I stopped in to see Rosalie, the owner of Marcello Travel.

"Are you interested in running ads for the holiday season?" I asked.

She said she was, and we started to chat.

"I've got a great bargain on a five-day Thanksgiving cruise," she said. "If you're interested I can get you a nice discount."

I started thinking about it and decided it would be a perfect getaway for Ryan and me. We'd be away from work, away from the boat and have nothing to focus on but each other. Maybe we could get back to what we once had.

That afternoon I called him at work and said, "Let's go out to dinner tonight. I've got something—"

He cut in before I had a chance to finish. "We've got to talk."

That was it. There was nothing more. Given the serious tone of his voice I thought maybe he was losing his job or one of the investment houses had burned to the ground.

THAT EVENING HE GOT HOME a few minutes after eight, later than if he'd come straight from work but earlier than he'd been coming home. I had the chicken noodle casserole already made and was keeping it warm in the oven.

"I thought you'd be earlier," I said. "Dinner's ready."

"I'm not hungry."

"It's chicken noodle casserole—"

"I want a divorce."

His words came at me like a shotgun blast. Of all the disasters I'd imagined, this was the one I hadn't expected. We'd weathered the worst of times, and now our relationship was nowhere near as contentious as it had been during my pregnancy.

When you hear something you don't expect, you tend not to believe it.

"What are you talking about?" I asked.

He looked square into my face and said, "I want a divorce. I'm sorry, but I just don't love you anymore."

This wasn't an argument. There was no yelling or screaming. There was not even the bristly sound of anger. His voice was flat and unemotional, which made it all the more painful.

I could deal with anger. In an argument we'd poke bitter barbs back and forth then move on to finding neutral ground, but this wasn't an argument. It was simply a statement of fact.

Later on I would think of a thousand different things I could have said, but at that moment all I could do was stammer, "Surely you're not serious?"

"Yes, I am. I've been thinking about this for a while and I've come to the realization that I just don't love you, so it's better…"

I could see the finality in his face. This was not a moment of anger, it was a decision he'd come to without ever consulting me. It was said with the same brittle, hard voice he'd used when he said he didn't want the baby.

Only now he was saying he didn't want me.

I turned away, walked into the bedroom and pulled the door closed behind me.

THE NEXT MOVE

Ophelia Browne once told me most of life's heartaches come from having the wrong expectations.

"People, for instance," she said. "You get a glimpse of them in one light and expect the whole to be like that one tiny little glimpse, but it seldom is."

She's right about that. In the darkest times of our being together, I kept thinking of Ryan as he was that first night when he took me to the Fourth of July fireworks. I stood his image right next to Daddy's and expected him to be the same. But he wasn't. Daddy was a man who loved his baby girl; he'd never dream of giving me away because he wasn't *established* enough. I should have seen that ugly side of Ryan when he couldn't find room in his heart for our baby, but I didn't and now I was going to pay the price.

As much as I hated Ryan, I hated myself even more. I hated myself for being stupid enough to believe he was like Daddy, and I hated myself for letting him be the master of my life. I let him be the one to decide everything. Absolutely everything. Not just what investments to buy, but when to get married and even when to start a family.

That night I decided I'd had enough. The next morning I

would leave this place. Walk out, and, God willing, never look back. I didn't need Mama or Ryan or anybody else to take care of me.

I'd take care of myself.

RYAN SLEPT ON THE SOFA that night, and in the morning I waited until he was gone from the house before opening the bedroom door. Once I was certain he was no longer there, I went into the kitchen to fix a cup of coffee and saw the stove still set on warm. I pulled the chicken noodle casserole from the oven and dumped it in the garbage, dish and all.

The previous night I'd cried for hours on end, but after I'd run out of tears it finally dawned on me: crying didn't change anything. If I didn't want to live with this kind of unhappiness, then the thing I had to change was me. When I finished my coffee, I went back to the bedroom, pulled my suitcases from beneath the bed and started packing.

It's funny how the things I'd once thought so important now didn't even warrant a second look. The only things I took were my clothes, a few books and the picture of Daddy and me that sat on the dresser. A framed picture of Ryan was right beside it, but I left that one behind.

It wasn't until I got behind the wheel of my car that I realized I had nowhere to go. With my suitcases piled in the trunk I spent the day driving around calling on customers, the same as always. Not once did I mention what had happened or let a tear come to my eye.

At four o'clock I called Nicole at the office and asked if she could meet me for a drink.

"I need some advice," I said.

We met at Taco Joe's, sat in a booth and ordered margaritas. As soon as the waiter left us alone with our drinks and a basket of corn chips I told her, "Ryan and I are getting a divorce."

She gulped down a swallow of margarita. "Did you say divorce?"

I nodded. "That's right." Every nerve in my body was tied in knots, but I was trying not to let it show. With the same unemotional tone Ryan used when he told me, I repeated, "He just doesn't love me anymore."

"That's bullshavicky!" Nicole said. "What's the real reason?"

"That's the reason he gave me. He looked me right in the eye and said he wanted a divorce because he doesn't love me anymore."

"Bullshavicky!" she repeated. "There's more to it than he's saying. My bet is he's having an affair."

"Ryan? I don't think so. He's too wrapped up in that boat, his buddies from work, watching over his investment proper—"

"Bullshavicky," she said again. "Bullshavicky" is Nicole's favorite word, and at times like this she let it fly loud and clear. A middle-aged woman sitting at the table across from us turned and gave her a look of annoyance.

I leaned across the table and whispered to Nicole, "Lower your voice."

She rolled her eyes and kept right on going. "Ryan's out for Ryan. He wouldn't leave you unless he had something better."

That thought hurt like hell, but I had to admit she was probably right.

The waiter came by, and we ordered a second round of drinks.

"You need a lawyer," Nicole said. "And you need to be quick about it, or he'll screw you out of everything."

"Like what? Some used furniture? Those old houses he's renting?"

Nicole raised her hand and rubbed her fingers together.

"Money. Whatever he's got, you're entitled to half of it."

"I don't want anything, I just want out. I've given up too much alrea—"

"More bullshavicky," she said, but this time she kept her voice a bit lower. "If you walk away and let him keep everything, then he wins. Is that what you want?"

I shook my head.

She tore a square off of the paper placemat, wrote something and handed it to me.

"Call this guy," she said. "He's the lawyer who handled Sissy's divorce, and he's good."

She'd scrawled a number on the scrap of paper and below it was a name: Leon McVey.

Nicole and I shared an order of chicken quesadilla and talked until after ten; then she suggested I bunk on her sofa for a while. I thanked her and said no. At some point between the second and third margarita, I'd come up with a plan.

THAT NIGHT I CHECKED INTO Babe's Motel out on State Highway 23. I knew Babe Wilson. She was one of my customers, and I'd gotten her good placement in the business-to-business tabloid supplement. When I told Babe I was going to be there for a while, she gave me the room next to hers and suggested I come by for coffee in the morning.

"I've always got a pot going," she said.

This might sound strange, but knowing she was right next door made me feel good. I had a place where I belonged. Not a house owned by Ryan or Mama, but a place of my own. It was a dinky little room with a bed, two nightstands and a dresser with a bottom drawer that wouldn't open, but none of that mattered. What mattered was that I'd taken the first step in what would prove to be a very long journey.

RYAN'S REASON

Leon McVey's office was on the second floor of a red brick building in downtown Wyattsville. The reception room had a single desk, a brown leather sofa and two-year-old magazines.

I approached the silver-haired woman at the desk and said, "My name is Cheryl Ann Carter; I'm here to see Mister McVey."

"Okay." Without moving from her seat, she turned toward the back office and yelled, "Leon, your two o'clock is here!"

Seconds later he stepped from his office into the reception area. He paused beside the receptionist, reminded her that she was supposed to use the intercom not holler, then turned to me and stuck his hand out.

"Leon McVey," he said.

"Cheryl Ann Carter," I replied and shook his hand.

"Pleased," he said and led me back to his office.

As we walked I told him, "Nicole Polanski suggested I talk to you."

"Yeah, she called this morning and told me you'd be coming in." He sat behind the desk and pulled out a note pad.

I took the chair in front. "I want to file for a divorce."

There is no way to describe how strange it felt to hear those words coming from my mouth, but all of a sudden I had an urge to explain.

"It's not actually me who wants the divorce, it's Ryan. Day before yesterday he came home and out of the blue said he didn't love me anymore." I stopped and started digging through my bag for a tissue.

"What did you do then?" McVey asked.

"I waited until the next morning, then I packed my bags and left."

His wrinkled face pinched into a grimace. "That's not good. You should've stayed and made him get out."

"Why?"

"With you leaving he'll claim you deserted him and argue to keep the house."

"So let him keep it. I don't want any part of him or his stuff."

"Whoa!" McVey said. "I know you're upset, but you've gotta be practical about this. You should get everything you're entitled to."

"I don't want it! Not the house, not those investment properties, not the boat, not even this damn ring!" I blinked back the tears blurring my vision and started struggling to remove the wedding band I'd worn for over a year. It was stuck.

"Try cold water and soap," McVey suggested. Without slowing for another breath, he said, "So tell me about the boat and these investment properties."

I explained that Ryan now had three houses rented out for more than the cost of the mortgages and a twenty-six-foot Lyman cabin cruiser docked at the Two Rivers Marina.

"But I don't want any of that stuff," I said. "All I want is out."

To hold the pieces of my broken heart together I'd decided that whatever I did I would do on my own; I was no longer going to be dependent on anybody. Dependency was nothing more than a welcome mat for disappointment.

"You're nuts," McVey said sharply. "You walk away with nothing, and the sleaze gets exactly what he wants."

I have to admit I liked hearing McVey call Ryan a sleaze. It was a strange sense of justification for the way I was feeling.

"All that stuff is in his name," I said. "So what can I do?"

McVey started scribbling notes on his pad. "You've gotta go at him with a demand for something. So decide what you want; then if he doesn't agree to the terms, I'll slap him with an injunction that puts everything in escrow until we battle it out in court. That means the rent money, use of the boat, everything is tied up until final settlement. Unless he's a real asshole, he's not gonna want that."

The thought of making Ryan miserable was somehow comforting. At first I thought of saying I wanted two of the rental properties, but the truth was I didn't. They were always in need of some repair or another and in neighborhoods I wasn't crazy about. Remembering Ryan's love of the boat, I figured losing that would be the thing that hurt most.

"I want the Lyman," I said.

"A boat? Not a house?"

I nodded. "Last summer there was a guy at the marina who said he'd be interested in buying it, so I think it would be pretty easy to sell."

McVey gave a dubious shake of his head and moved on.

I gave him all the information he needed: where Ryan worked, his Social Security number, the name of our bank and a lot of other seemingly insignificant details. He made note of everything.

When we neared the end of our conversation, McVey said, "I'm gonna check this dude out. My gut tells me there's more to this than meets the eye."

"I don't think so," I said. "We've gone through a rough patch, and he probably just got tired of the situation." I explained about giving up Baby Girl and how, despite all our trying, we'd not been able to have another baby.

"We'll see," McVey said. Then we shook hands, and he said he'd call as soon as he'd had a chance to look into everything.

I left his office happier than I'd arrived. There was an odd satisfaction in thinking I could conceivably take away the thing Ryan prized most. It seemed like poetic justice since he'd made me give up Baby Girl because of the damn boat.

A WEEK LATER I GOT a message from McVey. I called, and he asked me to come in.

"I've got something for you," he said.

I had appointments lined up for most of the day, so it was close to five when I got there. The woman wasn't at the reception desk, so I stood around for a minute or two then called out as she had.

"Hello there…"

Seconds later McVey stuck his head out. "Sorry. I was wrapping up a phone call."

I followed him back to his office, and we sat as we had before. He pulled a large manila envelope from the drawer and laid it on the desk.

"I was right," he said and pushed the envelope toward me. "This is why he wanted you out of the house."

I opened the envelope. Inside were pictures of Ryan and a girl who looked to be about fifteen. She had long blond hair and was quite obviously pregnant. He had his arm circling her waist the same way he did with me when we first moved to Burnsville. Tears filled my eyes as I sat there looking at those first two pictures.

"There's more," McVey said. He pushed those pictures aside and uncovered a third and fourth where the two of them were walking into our house. Ryan was carrying an unfamiliar suitcase—most likely hers.

"She looks pregnant," I said, stating the obvious.

"She is," McVey replied. "And from what I can gather it's his."

It's odd the things that come to mind at a time like this, but my next question was, "When is she due?"

"Sometime in January."

"That means he's been seeing her…"

McVey read my thoughts and nodded. "Seven months."

This thought made my blood boil. All the while I believed we were trying to have a baby and blamed myself for the failure, he was shacking up with somebody else and making a baby of his own. In that single moment I came to hate Ryan more than I'd ever thought possible.

"So," McVey said, "do you want to rethink what you want in this divorce settlement?"

"You bet I do!" I replied angrily. "I want the boat and a fifty percent buy out on all the investment properties."

McVey grinned. "Good. I'll also include he has to pay for all legal fees."

When I left his office that evening I knew Nicole had been right. McVey was exactly what I needed.

WHO GETS WHAT

My life had been one long stretch of leaning on other people. As a toddler I'm certain I leaned on Mama, but honestly speaking I can't remember such a time. I do remember being a young girl and looking to Daddy for almost everything. Once he was gone, I slid Ryan into that spot and leaned on him. Then when I got pregnant with Baby Girl, Ryan became emotionally unavailable and I leaned on Ophelia Browne. She gave me the wisdom and strength to get past what I had to do.

Now I was through with leaning on anybody. It was time I stood on my own two feet and learned to take care of myself. I didn't mean I wouldn't have friends, but I wasn't going to use those friends as leaning posts. That's for sure.

I didn't have to worry about doing it with Nicole; she was the kind of friend who'd smack me in the head and say, "Get a grip!" I needed more friends like her.

BY THE TIME MCVEY GOT the ball rolling, Ryan already had his own lawyer. Harold Sorenson was a man who stood a good six-

and-a-half feet tall and had a booming voice that could intimidate the devil himself.

Our first meeting was the week before Christmas in the conference room of Sorenson's office. When McVey and I walked in, Ryan was already sitting at the long table. He looked up at me and gave a smug smile. I walked by as if he were invisible and sat on the other side of the table, not directly opposite him, more towards the end.

Sorenson shook hands with McVey; then he sat and started the conversation.

"Although Cheryl Ann Carter abandoned the familial home, my client as a gesture of generosity is willing to offer $5,000 in exchange for her release on any and all claims to what she refers to as jointly owned properties," Sorenson said. "We feel this is a more than fair offer since my client is in fact the sole owner of these properties."

McVey chuckled and leaned back in his chair. "Fat chance," he said and laid the manila envelope on the table along with a folder stuffed full of papers. "We've got your boy dead to rights."

Sorenson eyed him with a dubious look. "Meaning?"

"We can start with the fact that Mister Carter gave my client no alternative but to leave because of his flagrant affair with an underage minor." He lifted the flap on the envelope and slid the pictures out onto the table.

Ryan's face turned red. "Shelby's eighteen, not underage."

McVey folded his arms across his chest and shook his head. "Not good enough. She turned eighteen two weeks ago. But judging from that bump in her belly I'd say you were screwing her when she was seventeen."

Ryan rolled his eyes and looked away.

"Let's not turn this molehill into a mountain," Sorenson said. "Our objective here is to come to some sort of settlement agreement, not argue about who's at fault."

"So you want to discuss finances?" McVey opened the folder. "Okay, then. In 1995 when they first moved in together, my client deposited $3,728 in their joint account." He handed a copy of the bank statement to Sorenson. "And in the three-plus years since then her earnings have exceeded his, which means that technically he has been living off of her."

He leaned forward, took a small sip from the glass of water in front of him, then continued.

"If we take a look at the first three quarters of this year alone..."—he paused just long enough to hand Sorenson another packet of statements—"...you'll see that my client has actually been the major contributor to the bank account that funded all of the purchases, including the Lyman cabin cruiser, the rental property on Washington Street, the rental—"

"Excuse me," Sorenson said. "I need a moment with my client."

He looked at Ryan and motioned for him to step outside the room.

"Hurry back," McVey said. "I've got more."

THEY RETURNED FIVE MINUTES LATER. Ryan had that pissed-off look I'd come to know only too well.

"Obviously this is not going to be a one-and-done deal," Sorenson said. "So let's talk about what your client wants. Then we can work on narrowing down an equitable percentage on the distribution of assets."

"Since your client has already ensconced his underage friend in the primary dwelling, my client feels it only fair she get the boat."

Ryan's back stiffened. "Not the boat!"

McVey ignored Ryan's outburst and turned to Sorenson. "If your client won't agree to this, I'll petition the court to hold all assets in escrow until the properties are appraised and percentage of ownership can be established."

"She just wants to sell it," Ryan snapped. "But that boat means something to me. I've put a lot of work into it!"

Before the meeting McVey had warned me not to say anything.

"You've got to realize they'll try to trick you into saying something they can use against you," he told me.

At the time I'd nodded and given my promise, but now I simply couldn't control myself.

"That's true, you have put a lot of work into the boat," I said angrily. "But maybe instead of playing around on it, you should have been working on your marriage!"

McVey turned and glared at me, so I ended my tirade and sat back.

"I appreciate the claim that your client put a lot of work into the boat," he said, "but my client put a lot of work into making their house a home. She's suffered a grievous wrong because of his actions. So where do we go from here?"

AFTER A TWO-HOUR SESSION OF back and forth claims and blames, it was finally agreed I got the boat but with the stipulation that if I wanted to sell it Ryan had the right of first refusal. The remainder of our holdings would be appraised at current value and divvied up on a 50-50 basis.

A SMALL WORLD

On Christmas Eve I moved out of Babe Wilson's motel and into the small cabin on the boat. Before the stores closed that evening, I went to K-Mart and bought a little twelve-inch screen TV. On the way back to the marina, I stopped and picked up two bottles of red wine and a bag of potato chips.

That night I sat in my tiny little cabin watching movies and trying to pretend it wasn't Christmas Eve. Shortly after nine a storm came through, and I sat there listening to the rain as I cried my heart out. I thought back on the Christmas after Daddy died and even though we didn't have even a sprig of pine or a lit candle, that miserable Christmas was way better than this one. At least I wasn't alone.

The loneliness of that night caused a shell to form around my heart, and I vowed I would never let anybody hurt me as Ryan had. The thing I didn't realize then was that in closing the door to heartache, I was also closing the door to love.

In that week between Christmas Eve and New Year's Eve, I became a different person. You can say such a thing is impossible, but I assure you it's not.

THE CABIN OF THE BOAT was livable but so tiny that if you turned quickly you'd bump into yourself. The stove consisted of two small burners and a microwave that took forever to reheat a mug of coffee. Below the stove there was a square box refrigerator large enough for a six-pack of beer, a bottle of wine and a chunk of cheese or some cold cuts. If you had a loaf of bread you had to squash it into the overhead. There was no countertop. None. The entire kitchen fit into three feet of space.

Everything in the cabin was compacted and made tiny. To use the shower, you had to flip the toilet seat down and sit; there wasn't room enough to stand.

There were no clothes closets, only cubbies. I could fit two or maybe three hangers on the single hook outside the bathroom door. Everything else had to be folded over again and again until it was small enough to fit in a cubby.

This was my new life, pared down to nothing but the bare necessities. You might wonder why I would choose to live this way. I did it not because it made me happy, but because my having the boat made Ryan miserable.

The old adage "Misery loves company" is truer than you might think. I was miserable and found a certain sweetness in making Ryan miserable also. In my mind he deserved every mean thing I could heap on him and more. He was the cause of a thousand heartaches that picked at my soul, and the thing at the top of my list was that he'd pushed me into giving up Baby Girl.

Taking the boat from him was my twisted version of revenge. I foolishly thought that making him unhappy was more important than making myself happy. The truth was I got no joy out of the boat. I didn't know how to operate it and wouldn't dare try to back it out of the slip, but I stayed there to spite Ryan.

ON CHRISTMAS DAY I PULLED a water-stained canvas tote from beneath the bunk, loaded it with toiletries, a towel and clean underwear, then headed for the marina clubhouse. The facilities at the yacht club were fairly nice, not luxurious but way better than sitting on the toilet while a trickle of lukewarm water sprayed my shoulders.

When I returned to the boat, I felt clean and refreshed. Determined not to sit around feeling sorry for myself, I got busy packing away the clothes I'd brought from the motel. There was barely enough room for a stack of jeans and tee shirts in the cubbies, so I hung two of the suits I'd use for work on the hook and packed the remainder back in the suitcase. For the time being I'd keep it in the trunk of my car.

Once that was done, I boiled some water, made myself a cup of tea and sat down to read *Angela's Ashes*. It was a dreary story, a book I normally would not have bothered with, but it was the only book on the boat. I flipped through the pages, glossing over words and capturing none of their intent. After rereading the same paragraph a dozen times, I set the book aside and snapped on the TV.

I clicked past one channel after another, but every station was celebrating Christmas. There were Christmas movies, talk shows about Christmas on the farm, glittering examples of Christmas in the city, chefs cooking up bountiful holiday dinners—a thousand reminders that it was Christmas, and I was sitting here alone with a half-empty bag of potato chips.

A CABIN NO WIDER THAN you are tall can be somewhat of a prison, so that evening I climbed out of the boat, pulled the hatch shut and walked back to the marina clubhouse. When I heard laughter coming from the bar I walked in, boosted myself onto a stool and ordered a beer. I looked like a single bookend, sitting alone and without purpose. The laughter I'd heard came from a group on the far side of the bar.

A blonde woman said something, and the crowd laughed louder. Minutes later the tall man at the center of the group caught my eye. He raised his arm and waved me over.

"Come join us!" he called.

I picked up my glass, walked over and stuck out my hand to introduce myself.

"Cheryl Ann Ferguson," I said, going back to the name I'd used for the first eighteen years of my life.

"Joe Montello," he replied.

From across the bar he'd looked younger, but up close I could see he was probably in his late fifties. He had a graying beard and a paunch that hung over his belt, but that wasn't what you noticed. The warmth of his smile was the thing that caught your eye.

"You live here?" he asked.

I nodded. "Now I do. East end of the dock, the twenty-six-foot Lyman."

"I'm two down from you. The 3650 Cruiser."

I knew the boat. It was half again the size of mine.

I finished my beer. Joe ordered a second one for me then introduced the others in the group. Mostly just first names.

People who live on boats come and go; a marina is not a place where you're likely to make lasting friendships. Some people you saw once and then they were gone. Others stayed a week, maybe two, then they too disappeared. Joe was one of the few who, like me, went nowhere.

Individually we were lonely people, people without a place to be or someone who cared; together we became part of a whole, a band of friends. I was one of them. I belonged. We drank, laughed, told off-color jokes and pretended it wasn't Christmas. This was the new me, the different me. The me who could no longer be hurt by Ryan or anyone else.

TWO DAYS AFTER CHRISTMAS I had my hair cut. Not the shoulder-length trim I usually got, but a sharp angular style that hugged the nape of my neck. That same day I bought two pairs of black jeans and four stretchy black tops. They suited my mood—dark and heavy.

I packed away my pink shirts and ivory-colored blouses. Wearing pastel shades made me vulnerable. Black was a powerful color, a suit of armor that made me feel less of a girl and more a force to be reckoned with. Black was the new me.

A NEW MILLENNIUM

The fourth of January was Baby Girl's second birthday. I thought about it all day and that evening drove over to Lawton just to cruise past the Stuart house, hoping to catch a glimpse of her. I knew by now she would be walking and talking, probably following LeAnn from room to room and calling out, "Mama."

I circled the block three times, and when I passed their house I slowed to a crawl. Inside the lights were on, and I could see people moving but they were nothing more than shadows because the window was covered with a lacy curtain. If I thought it would go unnoticed I would have parked on the street and stayed all night for a chance to see my baby, but the Stuarts lived in an area where cars were tucked away in garages at night and guests parked in the driveway. A lone car sitting alongside the curb would have been as obvious as a bonfire in the middle of the street.

AFTER NEARLY AN HOUR OF circling the block, I left and drove back to the marina. Joe Montello was at the clubhouse bar, so I went in and plopped down on the stool beside him.

"Crappy day," I said.

"It happens." Joe smiled and ordered me a Budweiser.

That night after a few beers at the clubhouse, we went back to Joe's boat and drank tequila until we were both blind drunk. He told me about the ex who was milking him for all he was worth. I told him about Ryan and how I hated myself for letting Baby Girl slip from my life.

"Today's her second birthday," I said, sobbing. "She should be with her mama."

"She is," he said solemnly. "And if you really love her you've got to accept it."

Drunken people seldom make sense, but Joe's answer was more sensible than any thought I'd had over the past two years.

"You're right," I whimpered and threw back another shot of tequila.

That night we slobbered tears on each other's shoulders and swore sooner or later things would get better. Sometime in the wee hours of the morning we gave up the tears and fell asleep, him on one bunk, me on the other. In the morning I woke to the smell of coffee.

There are times in life when everybody needs a friend like Joe. A friend who will listen without being judgmental; a friend who is right where you are and can feel the anguish in your heart.

FRIENDSHIPS YOU MAKE IN A bar are somewhat like disposable towels. You need them and you're thankful they're there, but you never expect them to last. This was a thing Joe and I both understood.

Throughout the months of January and February, we were best friends. It wasn't something planned; we just sort of happened upon one another. He was always there at the clubhouse bar, and I was always looking for a friend.

Joe wasn't my only friend; there was a whole group of us. All misfits of a sort. People with a first name and no last. In a single night we became best friends, and before the bar closed we'd be hanging on to one another like lifelong buddies.

The clubhouse bar was a place where no one had a past and no one cared about the future. We were all living for the moment, the right here and right now. Hugs were given freely, and parting was never sorrowful.

In early March Joe told me he was leaving at the end of the week.

"Heading over to the Bahamas," he said. "I've got friends there."

I wanted to grab onto his arm and hold him back, to say that he had friends here also, to say that I was his friend and didn't want him to go. But I couldn't. Ours wasn't that kind of friendship.

"Cool," I said and smiled. "Think you'll be coming back?"

He shrugged. "Depends." He didn't say on what.

THAT FRIDAY AFTER WORK I stopped in at the clubhouse. Joe wasn't there. I ordered a beer, drank it down quickly and left. As I headed back to the boat I passed the slip where Joe's 3650 had been. It was empty.

The weight of him leaving was heavy in my chest, but it was a luxury I couldn't afford to keep. I changed into my black jeans and returned to the clubhouse. The only person in the bar was a silver-haired man sitting alone. I walked over and sat on the stool next to him.

"Hi," I said and smiled. "Name's Cheryl Ann. You new here?"

He told me his name was William Potter. He was newly retired and working his way down the east coast.

"I'm figuring to spend summer on the boat then settle someplace in Florida," he said.

We spent the evening together, buying drinks for each other and talking about all the things we were going to do. I lied and he lied; then we hugged each other and went our separate ways. We both said, "Let's do this again tomorrow," but I didn't go back and I'm pretty sure he didn't either.

IT TOOK OVER A YEAR for the divorce to become final. The lawyers argued over everything imaginable. I was angry with Ryan and wasn't willing to budge an inch—not because I actually wanted any of those things, but because I didn't want him to have them. I wanted him to feel the pain of missing his prized possessions the same way I felt the pain of missing my baby girl.

In March of 2001 the decree came through. A few weeks later Ryan and his girlfriend were married; by then their son was over a year old.

I had been living on the boat for almost a year-and-a-half, although you would scarcely call it living. I did nothing more than sleep there. Being in that cabin was like living in a closet. I couldn't take a shower, cook a meal or have a friend over. It was a prison of my own making.

HATING SOMEONE FOREVER IS A difficult thing to do. It uses up all your energy and wears you down. It forces you to be someone and something you're not. You drink more and laugh louder just to prove you're happier than he is. You're the only one who cares about this, but you ignore that fact and continue. Sooner or later the weight of carrying such hatred becomes a burden too great to bear, and you start to realize that you're hurting yourself way more than you're hurting him.

ON THE SECOND SATURDAY OF April I called the house to tell Ryan I was ready to sell the boat and he could buy it back. His new wife answered the telephone.

"Is Ryan there?" I asked. I heard the shrill screams of a toddler in the background.

"He's working today," she said. "You can call him at the Fairmont Store." She hung up the receiver without ever asking who I was or what I wanted. I can't say whether she knew it was me or simply didn't care. There was an all-too-familiar weariness in her voice.

I called the Fairmont store and spoke with Ryan. It was the first civil conversation we'd had since the night he'd looked me in the eye and said he didn't love me anymore.

"I'm going to sell the boat," I said. "Are you still interested in buying it?"

There was a long silence, and for a moment I thought maybe he'd hung up.

"How much?" he finally said.

"Twelve thousand."

Again silence.

"Do you want it or not?" I asked.

"I want it," he said, "but I need a few weeks to get the money."

"Okay." I gave him the address of my post office box and said when I got the check I'd send the ownership papers.

DURING THE TIME I'D LIVED on the boat I'd made hundreds of new friends—old, young, some sober, some not so much. All of them had come and gone through my life with the intensity of a thunderstorm passing by on a hot summer day. Two weeks later, like many of those friends, I was gone from the marina.

The Apartment

You might think once a truckload of misery is dumped on you that you're destined to live with it forever, but that's not true. Just like everything else misery has an expiration date, and when it comes around you get to choose whether to leave it behind or hang on to it. I held on to mine for way too long.

I didn't call it misery; I called it freedom. I let it hide behind loud music, alcohol and the flimsy friendships of people who were little more than strangers. The day I drove out of the marina for that last time it was as if a bag of bricks had been lifted from my back.

AFTER BEING SQUEEZED INTO A cabin the size of a doll's house, I wanted space. A place with closets to hang clothes, a kitchen to cook meals, a bed not shaped like the bow of a boat, one where I could sit up without banging my head on the ceiling.

I LIKED MARGARET FOLEY THE moment I met her. She was a

plumpish woman with streaks of silver in her hair and the smell of cookies clinging to her.

When she opened the door I said, "I called about the apartment."

She pushed the door open and said, "Ah, yes, come sit for a few minutes. I've got cookies in the oven, and they're ready to come out."

"I can smell them," I said as I followed her through the hallway and into the kitchen. It was a cozy room with potted plants on the windowsill, plaid wallpaper and chintz curtains tied back with a ribbon.

"The apartment's upstairs," Margaret explained. "It's three-fifty a month including everything but a telephone. If you want a telephone, you can have one. The jack's already there but with not knowing who might come in—" She pulled the tray from the oven, waited a few moments, then one by one began transferring the cookies to a cooling rack. "You like cookies?"

"Love them."

She moved two of the warm cookies to a plate and set it on the table. "Try these."

I broke off a piece and stuffed it into my mouth. "Delicious," I garbled.

Once she had all of the cookies on the rack Margaret said, "Come, I'll show you through the apartment, then we'll have tea."

"Oh, no, that's really not—"

"I can make coffee if you'd prefer."

"Tea is fine," I said and followed her up the stairs.

The apartment was everything I wanted and more. The kitchen, a mirror image of the one downstairs, had the same plaid wallpaper, only this one was rose-colored rather than blue. I could already imagine chintz tiebacks at the window. Every room was freshly painted, the larger bedroom in pink, the smaller one in the palest yellow imaginable.

"I love it," I said with a sigh as we walked from room to room.

"Lots of closets," she said and opened one door after another.

We circled through the rooms and came back to the kitchen. "The laundry center is here..." She pulled open a set of double doors to show the washer and dryer sitting side by side.

"It's small," she said apologetically, "but quite efficient."

Before we started down the stairs I was already thinking of what kind of furniture I'd need.

We returned to her kitchen, and as I sat there having tea and cookies I could feel a new kind of happiness sprouting inside my soul.

WITH THE MONEY RYAN PAID for the boat still warm in my pocket, I went furniture shopping. This time I bypassed the Salvation Army store and headed for Baker Brothers, a furniture gallery where Mister George, the sales manager, dashed over to greet you the minute you stepped through the door.

I spent almost ten thousand dollars that afternoon and got one hundred thousand dollars' worth of pleasure in doing it. I felt like Missus Vanderbilt pointing my finger at this sofa and that chair, then matching them to end tables and lamps. When I finished picking out furniture for the living room, I moved on to the bedroom.

I'd always thought a bed was simply a bed, but after I followed Mister George through the Sleep Center Gallery I knew better. With him standing beside me I kicked off my shoes and began testing out mattresses. After almost two hours of mattress testing and studying one room after another, I selected a pale ash queen-size bed with a six-foot-long dresser and two nightstands. I finished off my shopping spree with a round table and four captain's chairs for the kitchen.

Once he'd made note of everything, Mister George escorted

me to the Customer Courtesy Lounge and had his assistant bring us cups of coffee while he sat writing up the order.

"You can expect delivery in six to eight weeks," he said.

"Six weeks?" I said. "That's too long."

I'd already turned the boat over to Ryan and the apartment had nothing but carpeting and appliances. The only things I'd brought with me were a bunch of plastic bags filled with clothes and a twelve-inch television.

"Everything comes from the factory," he explained. "It's made to order."

There was several minutes of back and forth negotiations, but after I'd made clear my predicament we came to a compromise. The next day Baker Brothers delivered a truckload of discontinued floor sample furniture for me to use until my special order furniture came through.

That night when I stretched myself out on a real bed I thought I'd died and gone to heaven. I plumped both pillows beneath my head and lay there watching Jay Leno interview Rodney Dangerfield. It's funny how a simple thing like laughing along with the television can change the way you look at life.

MOVING INTO THAT APARTMENT WAS the start of me getting back to the person I once was. In the evening I'd come home from work and settle in with no desire whatsoever to go carousing. Little by little I began to discover the things I had once enjoyed: listening to music, crocheting and reading. Two years earlier I'd given up on *Angela's Ashes*, and then I'd just quit reading altogether. I can't even remember why. Maybe I'd forgotten how comforting the feel of a book in your hand can be.

Then one evening I came home and found a copy of John Grisham's novel *A Painted House* on the steps leading to my apartment. Margaret had left it for me. She did things like that.

Almost every day I'd come home and find some nice little surprise: a ripe tomato, a loaf of her banana bread, a plate of cookies. Sometimes there was a note, sometimes not.

On this night there was. "Read this book," it said. "You'll love it."

For almost two years I dreaded being alone in that dreary little cabin; now I didn't mind being by myself at all. I think it's because I no longer felt alone. If I felt the least bit lonely I could call down and invite Margaret up for a cup of tea or telephone Ophelia and talk for an hour.

Alone and lonely aren't the same thing. Margaret and Ophelia were both widows who lived alone but neither of them was lonely. They had friends and neighbors who cared about them. They had me. And now I had them. Plenty of times I'd been with a crowd of people talking and laughing at the clubhouse, and yet I still felt lonely. This was different. Being alone was okay because I wasn't lonely.

That evening I fixed myself an omelet for supper and sat at the table with the book propped in front of me. The story was a tale told by a boy who called his grandpa Pappy. As I turned the pages I got to know the boy and his family. Then I began to care about the boy. And then I grew fearful for him. I read straight through until one o'clock in the morning, and the next day I hurried home from work to finish the book. As I turned the last page I gave a sigh and decided to join the library.

THIS WAS THE SECOND NEW me, a person who in some ways resembled the first me. This time, though, I was a bit braver, a bit more determined to take on life and not buckle under the weight of it.

THE LETTER

B efore I was in the apartment three months, I had chintz curtains at the kitchen window and three potted plants sitting on the sill. They were plants I'd grown myself, with Ophelia's help of course.

She had an almost magical way of growing things. Ophelia could stick a seed in the ground and a few days later she'd have a full-grown plant. One time I told her I could smell the flower garden even before I rounded the corner of Haber Street.

"That's your mind racing ahead of your nose," she said, laughing. "You're reaching out for the fragrance you expect to find."

"No, no," I insisted. "There's something about this place, the house, the garden, even the apothecary. If not magic, how can you explain a potpourri that changes scent or a tea that makes people feel better?"

She gave a saddened smile. "I've always believed the magic of Memory House was something Edward and I created when we first moved in here." She went on to say how they'd had only a little furniture but a whole lot of dreams.

When she spoke of lying on the grass and looking up at the stars, it reminded me of that Fourth of July summer when Ryan and I did the same thing.

"I guess sometimes the dream thing works out, and sometimes it doesn't," I said wistfully.

Ophelia knew all about Baby Girl. She'd gone through it with me, and I'd shared every gory detail. Times when I thought my heart would burst open from the anguish, this is where I'd come. No matter how low I was Ophelia lifted me up so that I could see myself moving from one day to the next.

"You're still missing that baby, aren't you?" she said.

I nodded. "For almost nine months she was part of me and now she's gone—"

Ophelia interrupted. "She's not gone at all. She's living a fine life with a mama who loves her to pieces."

Back in the days of my pregnancy LeAnn and I had both come to the apothecary in search of dandelion tea. It dawned on me that she might still do so.

"Have you seen LeAnn?" I asked. "Have you seen Morgan?"

Ophelia gave a barely perceptible nod.

"Yes and yes," she said softly. "But Morgan and her mama deserve to have their own happiness. You gave LeAnn the greatest gift she'll ever have. Now you have to back away and let her enjoy that gift."

I knew Ophelia's words were true, but it was a thing easier said than done.

"I'm not going to interfere with their life," I said. "I'd just like a glimpse of Morgan, you know, to see if she has my smile or my eyes. She's gone, but I still feel there's this connection..."

"That's perfectly normal." She smiled and took my hand in hers. "You *are* connected to her. It's the same as the way God is connected to this earth, and the way I'm connected to every seed I plant. We're creators and we love our creations, but that doesn't mean we can hang on to them forever. Every plant that leaves here has a piece of me in it, but I don't expect the owner to bring it back every few weeks so I can watch it grow bigger."

I laughed at the analogy. "You're right. I know you're right."

Nothing more was mentioned that day, but two weeks later I found an envelope in my mailbox. It was a letter from LeAnn. It said Morgan was doing fine and was going to start kindergarten that fall. The letter indicated that she'd had some digestive issues the first two years, but by the time she was three they'd pretty much disappeared. Along with the letter there was a picture of my Baby Girl.

She had a wide grin on her face, and I could see an empty spot where her front tooth had fallen out. She had the same blue eyes and crooked smile as I did. I framed that picture and set it on my six-foot long dresser.

I can't say if Ophelia suggested LeAnn send that picture or conjured up some magic spell that caused her to do it. What I can say is that I was truly grateful. I treasured that little picture more than anything else I owned.

AS SUMMER TURNED TO FALL and the frost of winter settled in, I continued to visit Ophelia. I came almost every weekend. Some Saturdays I'd rap on Margaret's door and ask if she'd like to join me. She almost always answered yes and generally had a plate of cookies or some sort of cake to bring.

Once we were there Ophelia would brew a pot of dandelion tea, and the three of us would sit on the back porch talking like we were lifelong friends. It's funny because I was in my early twenties at the time, and while Ophelia and Margaret were both a good fifty years older than me it didn't seem to make a difference. When we were knee deep in conversation, it was as if I was the same as them.

About two weeks before Christmas Ophelia showed us a new treasure she'd found at the Sisters of Mercy thrift shop. It was a little pink rubber ball.

"Why, that's nothing but an old Spaldeen," Margaret said. "Those things used to be a dime a dozen."

"This one has memories attached to it," Ophelia replied.

Margaret laughed. "You've been had. That's a plain old Spaldeen."

"It may look the same as others," Ophelia countered, "but I can feel the memories in this one."

I leaned in closer and asked, "What memories?"

Ophelia had a faraway look in her eyes when she spoke; it was as if she was seeing what she was describing.

"It belonged to a troubled little boy," she said. "I think he was an orphan and the only things he had were a dog and this ball."

Margaret lifted the ball from Ophelia's hand and examined it carefully. "Most every boy had a Spaldeen at some time or another. You figured out the dog part because the ball's got teeth marks on it." She hesitated then added, "But I don't see anything to indicate he was an orphan."

"It's not something you see," Ophelia said. "It's just something I sense."

As she told how the boy would thunk the ball against the wall while he was worrying over what to do, Margaret just sat there looking skeptical.

Me, I believed anything was possible with Ophelia. She was a woman with talents beyond what the mind could imagine.

TWO WEEKS LATER THE THREE of us were sitting in the exact same spot when Margaret reached into her big satchel handbag, pulled out a music box and set it on the table. She looked over at Ophelia with a double-dare grin and asked what memories could be found in that.

"I didn't say I could find memories in everything," Ophelia replied. "Just in certain treasures."

"Harrumph," Margaret grunted. "I had a feeling you were just pulling my leg."

"I was doing no such thing!" Ophelia replied indignantly. "Certain memories get left behind by their owner, and they need someone to care for them so they don't fade away."

Not looking the least bit convinced, Margaret snatched up the music box and as she did so the box began to tinkle the tune of *Always*. She pulled her hand back as if it had been scalded and gasped.

"Impossible," she declared. "Edna's music box hasn't worked since the day she died."

"Maybe moving it around caused something to loosen up," I said.

Margaret jumped right over that suggestion and looked to Ophelia. "Did you do something?"

Ophelia shook her head ever so slowly. "No, but I'm real sorry about your sister."

Margaret just sat there with her mouth hanging open. Then she told us the story of the little sister who died when she was ten years old.

THE FLAT TIRE

I met Nick Lombardi the following summer. It wasn't planned. You can't plan stuff like that because when you do it never works out.

It happened on a Friday afternoon. I'd just finished my meeting with Ridgefield Trust and was on my way to meet Nicole at the Bronze Bull in Wyattsville. As I started toward my car I noticed it listing to the right.

Don't tell me...

I circled around to the back of the car and, sure enough, the back tire was folded over like a deflated balloon.

I know how to change a tire. I've known how to change a tire since before I left Spruce Street. But today I was wearing my light blue silk dress. It was not something I wanted to soil, and besides I was in somewhat of a hurry. I whipped out my cell phone and called Triple A.

"I've got a flat tire," I reported. "Can you send someone to change it?" I gave the gal on the phone my location, and she told me they'd have someone there in a half-hour or less.

"Please try to make it faster," I said and mentioned an appointment, leaving out that it was meeting a girlfriend for drinks.

"I'll do what I can," she promised. She told me that since I was on a downtown street I needed to stay with the car and flag the mechanic down when I spotted his truck.

I did as she asked, and in less than five minutes the tow truck came rumbling down Central Boulevard. I stepped into the street and waved him over.

The truck pulled to one side, and the driver climbed down from the cab of his truck. You'd have to be blind not to notice he was tall and good-looking. He wore mirrored sunglasses, so I couldn't see his eyes until he was standing next to me. Using his index finger he slid the glasses down his nose and looked over the top.

"Got a problem?" he said. He had a nice voice, deep but with a mellow sound.

For a few seconds I just stood there looking at his eyes. They were gorgeous, dark brown with the kind of lashes most women would kill for.

"Um, I've got a flat tire," I finally said.

He gave this funny little half-smile. "So, are you asking me to change it?"

"Of course," I answered. To me it seemed pretty obvious that if I called and asked for help I would expect him to change the tire, not just evaluate it.

"It's not that I don't know how to change a tire," I explained. "I do. But I'm meeting a friend, and I don't want to get dirty."

"No problem," he said. "Have you got a spare?"

I nodded and popped the trunk. He unfastened the spare, set it on the curb, then took the tire iron and began loosening the wheel bolts.

"So, where are you meeting this friend?" he asked.

"Wyattsville."

"Boyfriend?"

That's when I realized he was flirting with me.

There are times when it feels good to have a man notice you. It can be something as insignificant as a stranger on the street who turns to take a second look, but you somehow feel a bit more special for having commanded that moment. Trust me, any woman who says she doesn't appreciate that kind of attention is a flat out liar.

I flirted back. "No boyfriend. It's a gal I used to work with."

He took off his sunglasses and smiled, then slid the jack under the car and pumped it up. The easy way he moved made the work seem effortless. He said his name was Nick Lombardi and he'd come here from Baltimore. I gave him my name and said I worked for the Burnsville *Tribune*.

We chatted the whole time he was working. When he finished he lifted the flat tire into the trunk, then just stood there smiling at me as he wiped his hands with the rag he'd pulled from his back pocket.

It was an awkward moment, the kind where you feel you're supposed to say or do something but you're unsure of what. I started to wonder if maybe this wasn't a free service after all.

"Do I owe you something?" I asked.

He laughed. "Nope, not a thing." Then he gave me the sexiest smile imaginable, climbed back into his truck and drove off.

I stood there for a moment watching the tow truck disappear down the street; then I got into my car and headed for Wyattsville.

Halfway there my cell phone rang. I answered the call, and it was that same gal from Triple A.

"Our driver says he can't find your car," she said. "Are you sure of the location you gave me?"

"Huh? I think you're calling the wrong customer. Your mechanic has already been there and changed my tire. I'm back on the road."

"Hold on," she said.

Twenty seconds later she was back. "It wasn't our guy. He just got there."

"Well, then who…?"

"Beats me," she said. "So should I cancel the work order?"

"Yes, cancel it," I replied and laughed.

OF COURSE ONCE I TOLD Nicole the story she about peed her pants laughing.

"So you flagged some guy down, got him to change your tire and didn't pay him?"

"That's pretty much it," I said with a grin. "I offered, but he said no."

WE'D BOTH HAD TWO GLASSES of wine when I thought I saw him come in. He stopped just inside the door, looked the room over and then headed back toward our table.

Nicole had her back to the door, but I was face to face with him when he stopped, looked down and said, "Hi."

She did a head jerk turn and glanced up. "Well, hello yourself."

"Nicole, this is Nick," I said. "Nick is the guy who changed my tire."

She laughed and stuck out her hand to shake the one he offered. "So you're the guy who was not with Triple A."

"Yep, that's me."

He gave a smile that caused me to blush.

"I'm so embarrassed," I said. "I really did think you were the mechanic from Triple A. I had just called and then—"

"Don't worry about it," he replied in an offhanded way that made him even more likable.

"Let me at least buy you a drink," I offered.

"You've got a deal." He dropped down in the seat beside me.

Before the evening was over, Nick and I had dinner plans for the next night.

⌘

IT WAS EASY TO FALL in love with Nick Lombardi. There was nothing to not like about him. He was good looking, thoughtful and easy to be with. He knew all the right things to say and do. On our first date he took me to Le Brittney, a restaurant with candles on the table and waiters who appeared and disappeared with the flick of a finger.

As we sat there sipping our wine, he leaned toward me with the hint of a smile. His mouth was tilted slightly on one side and his eyes full of mischievous suggestions.

"You know this is going to turn into something," he said, giving his voice an almost whispery quality and keeping his eyes fixed on mine.

I could guess at what he meant, but I wanted to stay in the moment and keep the conversation going.

"So, what is it that you imagine will turn into something?" I asked playfully.

"I think you already know," he said, and his smile deepened. He stretched his arm across the table, traced his index finger along the bridge of my nose and then touched it to my lips. "It's us. We're going to be something special."

I'm certain I blushed because I felt the warmth in my cheeks. I think right then I knew I was destined to fall in love with Nick Lombardi.

NICK WAS IN HIS EARLY forties, but he didn't look it. He was muscular, well built and had the sexiest smile I'd ever seen. From the far side of a room he could look at me and smile as if he was seeing me naked, stripped down to my innermost thoughts. I knew the age difference was there, but I didn't think of what it meant long term. I took each day as it came and enjoyed it for what it was.

THE MIRACLE

The following November I took Margaret out to lunch on a Saturday, and as we were lingering over coffee I asked if she would have any objections to Nick moving in with me.

"As long as he doesn't smoke, I've no objection," she said, but I noted a bit of hesitation hanging on to her words.

"Are you sure?" I asked.

"I'm not your mama," she said, "but if I was I'd say you ought to think about marrying before you have him move in."

"We are thinking about it," I told her. "But not just yet." I explained how difficult the divorce from Ryan had been and how it had stretched out for more than a year.

"This time I want to be absolutely certain before I step into something I can't get out of."

Margaret nervously rearranged her napkin in her lap and then looked up.

"I just don't want to see you get hurt," she said. "If you honestly believe he can make you happy, then I'll be happy for you."

I leaned across the table and gave her hand an affectionate squeeze. "I have no doubt he'll make me happy."

We sat there and talked for almost two hours. I told her how thoughtful Nick was, how he'd hold the car door open for me, bring me flowers and take me to dinner at the loveliest restaurants. I didn't mention the one negative, because in my mind it wasn't all that much of a problem.

NICK MOVED IN THE WEEK before Thanksgiving. He came with two duffle bags and an armful of roses, a bouquet for me and another for Margaret. When he tapped on her door, thanked her for having him and handed her the flowers, she had a smile that stretched from ear to ear. I think she was happy for me and happy for herself also.

As I've said Nick was easy to love; he always had a smile and an ear willing to listen. He could tell a joke, sing a song or dance the shoes off your feet. And at night when we'd climb into bed together, he made love to me as if I were the only woman on earth.

After only a few days I knew I hadn't made a mistake this time. Ours was the kind of relationship I had always wished for. With Nick there was no pretense. We actually enjoyed the same things: smooth jazz, good books, rainy days and lazy mornings of cuddling beneath the comforter. That winter we spent most of our Sundays curled end to end on the sofa listening to Amy Winehouse or Kenny G and thumbing through the pages of a book.

Every day seemed like another perfect little helping of life. We lived for that day and enjoyed every moment of it. There was never a thought of wanting anything more than what we had.

PERHAPS SOMEWHERE IN THE BACK of our minds we both knew it

could happen, but neither of us believed it would. Before Nick moved in we'd discussed it.

"I'm forty-four years old," he'd said. "That's too old to be starting a family."

"Don't worry."

I explained that for almost a year after I'd given up the baby, Ryan and I tried to have another one.

"Unsuccessfully," I added. "He wasn't the problem, I was. Before I left the house, he had his new girlfriend pregnant."

The thought of this made me teary-eyed but not because I still loved Ryan. I had moved on where he was concerned; I no longer cared about him. I didn't even love him enough to hate him. But losing Baby Girl had left a forever hole in my heart.

"I wish I could have another baby," I said sadly. "But I doubt I ever will. Apparently God has decided that since I gave the first baby away, I don't deserve a second one."

At the time Nick said all the right things. He was sympathetic. Understanding. He said not to blame myself. He even pulled out the old tried-and-true "Everything happens for a reason." And at the end of the day we agreed that simply having each other would be enough.

IN JULY MY PERIOD WAS late. A few days one way or the other was not much of a concern. But a few days grew into a week and then two weeks. Even then I thought it unlikely I was pregnant, but to rule it out I bought one of those home pregnancy tests.

That evening after dinner I disappeared into the bathroom and watched in amazement as the stick turned blue. Even though I knew Nick's feelings about this, I returned to the living room with a goofy-looking smile on my face.

"Are you okay?" he asked.

"Better than okay," I said. "I'm pregnant."

He looked at me with the wide-eyed expression of shock and fear people often get when they've been stabbed with a knife or shot through the heart.

"I thought you said you couldn't—"

"I didn't think I could," I cut in. I pulled my hand from behind my back and showed him the stick. "See, blue. It's a miracle."

Nick was still sitting there with that gunshot look. He took a deep breath and spoke in slow, evenly spaced words.

"I can't do this," he said. "You knew, Cheryl. You knew up front how I felt about having a family." He lowered his face into his hands and shook his head as morosely as I've ever seen a man do.

"A baby is a huge responsibility," he added with a groan, "more than I'm capable of handling."

For the remainder of that evening we didn't speak ten words to one another. I think we were both waiting for the shock of my announcement to settle. Each of us needed time to get through our own thoughts.

I know what was in my mind; I was hoping Nick would change his. I was certain beyond a shadow of a doubt that I would never consider giving this baby up. The pain of losing Ryan was long gone, but the pain of losing my Baby Girl was still with me. Never again, I vowed. Never again.

I loved Nick, loved him dearly. He made me happy. He made me feel loved. He gave me a million reasons to smile and sing and dance. A million reasons to feel joyful. Still, if push came to shove and I had to choose between him and my baby, this time I would choose my baby.

AND THUS IT WAS

For the next three or four months there was little said about my pregnancy, but the easiness of our being together seemed to slip away. Not all at once but inch by inch. While in the earlier months we made love several times a week, it was now only on occasion and when I was in my sixth month it stopped altogether.

Nick remained thoughtful and considerate, but now instead of flowers he'd come home with a Dairy Queen Frosty, which was what I craved. I continued to work, and he continued to wake me each morning with a slide-by kiss and a cup of coffee. We even stayed with our routine of spending Sunday morning lying lazily in bed, but now I was on my side of the bed and he was on his. Between us there was generally a pile of books and newspapers.

I think we both knew what would happen, but the time would come soon enough and until then we would simply enjoy each other's company. I know this sounds strange to say, but it was almost like a metamorphosis. We went from being lovers to being friends. Maybe it was because we both understood friends can part without the terrible heartache that haunts lovers when they go their separate ways.

IN FEBRUARY I TOOK NICK out to dinner to celebrate his birthday. Instead of going to an intimate French restaurant as we used to do, he chose a steakhouse with a well-lit interior and great food. That evening was the first time we discussed what we both knew would happen.

"I'm forty-five years old," he said solemnly. "That's too old to be having babies. I love you, Cheryl Ann, but..."

I reached across the table and took his hand in mine.

"I love you too," I said, "but I gave up my first little girl, and I've never gotten over it. I can't let myself make the same mistake again."

"I wouldn't ask you to," he offered.

I gave a saddened laugh. "I couldn't. Motherhood does something to a woman's heart. Makes it bigger and more capable of loving, I suppose."

He smiled at my words.

"The love a mother feels for the baby growing inside of her is overwhelming, bigger than anything you can possibly imagine." I stopped and rearranged the silverware on the table, moving the knife and fork until they were perfectly aligned.

"With my first baby I was young and frightened. I thought I could never make it on my own. Now things are different. I'm older and stronger. I'll do whatever I have to do to keep this baby safe and give her a good home."

"It's a girl?"

I nodded. I'd known for almost a month that my baby was a girl, and this time the ultrasound had shown there were no abnormalities.

"I guess God decided to give me a second chance at being a mother, and this time I'm determined not to screw it up," I said.

"That's nice." Nick looked across the table, and in his eyes I could see both gloom and admiration. "I'm happy for you, Cheryl, but I'm sad for myself."

He was on the verge of saying something more, but the waitress came and set two platters of steak in front of us. As she prattled on asking if we wanted steak sauce, catsup or any other thing, I could almost see Nick's words drifting away.

Some things are probably better off left unsaid. That night I went home believing there was a thimble-sized grain of hope that once Nick saw the baby and held her in his arms, he would be swept away by the same kind of parental love I felt.

☙❧

THE DAYS AND WEEKS MOVED on, but Nick did not. In fact he became more thoughtful than ever. When I began to prepare for the baby, he gave the small yellow room a fresh coat of paint and assembled the crib.

In the last month of my pregnancy he even took over all the cooking. Every night when I came in from work, I'd smell something sizzling on the stove. After dinner we'd sit together on the sofa, me at one end, him at the other. More often than not my legs would be draped across his lap, and he'd be massaging my swollen ankles.

We had all the earmarks of a happily married couple eagerly awaiting the arrival of their first child, except I knew we weren't.

All the small signs were there. The wistful look in his eyes when I stepped from the shower naked and he saw the full blossom of my belly. The slump of his shoulders when he passed by the growing stack of pink and white baby blankets. Every day there was some new thing added: a rocking chair, a car seat, a changing table, all of it in preparation for her arrival and conceivably his departure.

Nick grew quieter and more withdrawn as the days narrowed to less than a handful. The night before I went into labor, he held me in his arms and kissed me as tenderly as you would a baby.

"I hope you know how much I love you," he whispered. "How much I'll always love you."

He didn't say it, but that night I heard the sound of goodbye in his words.

IN THE PRE-DAWN OF MORNING, when there was barely a glimmer in the sky, I felt the first stab of pain. My back had begun to ache hours earlier and I'd tossed and turned, unable to get to sleep. I waited until there was a second pain and then a third before I nudged Nick's shoulder.

"It's time," I said. "I think I'm starting labor."

"Okay," he answered and rolled out of bed.

Fifteen minutes later we were on our way to the hospital.

VIOLET WAS BORN AT 2:37 that afternoon. I named her after the color I'd seen in Ophelia's eyes. I hoped she would be like Ophelia, gentle, kind, loving and wise. I wanted her life to be as magical as I imagined Ophelia's to be.

Nick was beside me the whole time. He held my hand, wiped my brow and allowed my pain to become his. When she was placed on my belly still covered with mucous and streaked with my blood, he bent and whispered that she was beautiful.

The look on his face was as prideful as that of any new father, and for a brief moment I thought perhaps he would stay and come to love her as I did.

TWO WEEKS LATER NICK WAS gone. It happened on a Sunday. I'd

gotten up early because I heard Violet whimpering and thought she needed to be fed. I went to the nursery, lifted her into my arms and held her to my breast. We sat in the rocker, which creaked back and forth as she hungrily sucked my nipple.

I can't say how much time passed. An hour, maybe two. Once she drifted off to sleep again I tucked her back into the crib and returned to the bedroom. Nick was tossing the last of his things into the second duffle bag; the first one was already filled and tied.

"You're leaving?" I said.

He nodded. "I have to. The longer I stay, the harder it will be."

"Maybe if you stay long enough you'll lose the desire to go."

He stopped and looked across at me. "It's possible I would. But that wouldn't be the best thing for you, me or Violet. I'm too old, Cheryl. I'm set in my ways and too selfish to share you with a baby."

"But she's your baby too."

He turned back to the duffle bag and continued packing. "I don't want her. I'm not cut out to be a father. You knew from the start—"

"Yes, but I thought once—"

"You thought wrong." He slung one duffle over his shoulder, tucked the other one beneath his arm and walked past me without stopping.

"Nick..."

I heard the apartment door click shut then peeked from behind the curtain and watched as he left the house.

He popped open the trunk of his car, tossed the two bags in, then slammed it shut. Before he climbed into the car he stood there looking back at the house. I can't say for sure he was crying, but I believe he was. He gave his head a sorrowful shake, then swiped his cheeks with the back of his hand and climbed into the car.

After he drove off I stood there for several minutes looking at the empty parking spot. When a white Pontiac came and backed into the spot, I turned and went back to the nursery.

I lifted Violet into my arms and again sat in the rocker. I knew that now it was just me and my tiny little angel. When she began to fuss I pushed the chair back and forth and sang softly.

"Hush, little baby, don't say a word; Mama's gonna buy you a mockingbird…"

WORKING MOM

At times it seemed as if my life was one long, drawn-out succession of wrong choices and starting over. Now here I was, starting over yet again, this time with a baby who would depend on me for everything.

You might think this would be a daunting situation, but it wasn't. Yes, I knew I would miss Nick. I had grown used to turning in my sleep and finding him beside me. I'd grown used to having the comfort of his shoulder beneath my head. But for four long years I'd lived with the heartache of losing Baby Girl and when I weighed one against the other, I knew deep down I wanted to be a mother even more than I wanted to be a wife.

With only three weeks of maternity leave left, I had to make the most of every minute. Violet went wherever I went. After she was fed, diapered and dressed, I buckled her into her carry seat and off we'd go.

My first challenge was to find a daycare center. All too soon my leave would be up, and I had to have someone who would care for Violet. Not just a place that would take infants but a place that would nurture her and help her grow. We spent five afternoons visiting daycare centers before we found Sara's Playpen.

Sara specialized in babies and toddlers, the children most daycares shied away from. The problem was that Sara's Playpen was small and near capacity.

The day we visited, Sara had one of the babies in her lap. She sat in a rocking chair similar to mine, creaking back and forth just as I did. I liked that. I also liked Sara. She had a soft voice, and the room was meticulous, clean and bright. Each of the three cribs lined against the wall had the baby's nametag attached to the side bars.

"I have to return to work in two weeks," I said. "I'm hoping you can find room for Violet."

Sara gave me an apologetic smile. "We're full up. I only take three newborns at a time and as you can see..." She gave a nod toward the three cribs lined against the wall.

After seeing the other daycares, I was desperate to put Violet here where there was someone to hold her and rock her as I would.

"Please," I said. "I'm a single mom. I have to work. She's my only child. Isn't there—"

"Isaac is almost six months," Sara said. "He'll be moving to the intermediate room, but not for another three weeks and until then..."

I jumped on it. "Will you take Violet in three weeks?"

"If you don't mind waiting."

"Not at all," I replied enthusiastically.

I hurriedly filled out the paperwork and gave the bookkeeper a check for the first week. As we walked out the door Violet woke, and although they say such a thing is impossible at three weeks old I could swear she gave a sigh.

Once I had nailed down a daycare spot for Violet, I began to show her off to my friends. We had lunch with Nicole, visited the classified department gals and spent an afternoon at the apothecary.

Two minutes after we arrived Ophelia turned the sign on the apothecary door to "Closed," and the three of us sat on the back porch enjoying the fresh air. It was a perfect day, splatters of warm sunshine dancing across the floor and a light breeze that carried the scent of new mown grass.

Ophelia sat in the wicker chair, and I placed Violet in her arms. She was near eighty at the time, but cuddling the baby gave her the glow of a young mother.

"Violet has your eyes," she said and lovingly traced a crooked finger along the edge of the baby's chin.

I told her Nick was gone and explained all that had happened.

"I thought he would change his mind once he saw her and held her in his arms," I said, "but he didn't. He left without ever really getting to know her."

Ophelia hesitated, waiting for the melancholy sound of my words to fade away. She looked at Violet and then back to me.

"Perhaps it's for the best," she said. "A man unwilling to accept his own child has a selfish heart. There's no wisdom or compassion in a selfish heart; it beats only for itself. You expected him to be more than he was capable of being."

I understood the wisdom of Ophelia's words and tried to hold them in my heart so that in the dark of night when I ached to feel Nick's arms around me I could remind myself I had made the right decision.

THOSE LAST FEW WEEKS BEFORE I returned to work were filled with magical days of holding Violet to my breast, watching her grow and seeing the changes that came with each day. Although much of her time was still spent sleeping, she was starting to coo and gurgle happily.

The days were wonderful, but the nights were long and

lonely. I kept remembering Ophelia's words, but I also remembered the feel of Nick's mouth against mine and the weight of his arm across my waist as we slept curled together.

It is said that a woman's heart has many chambers and while the part that for so long ached to hold Baby Girl was now filled to overflowing, the other side, the side that gives itself to a man, was now empty.

Empty, yes, but not filled with agony as it was when I left Ryan. I missed Nick, but I had no hatred for him. He simply was who he was. He had never lied. This time the fault had been mine. I expected more than he could give.

I RETURNED TO WORK THE week before Violet had her spot at Sara's Playpen, and Margaret happily volunteered to be my babysitter for the week. She had a bad knee and one blind eye, but those things weren't enough to dissuade her.

"Are you sure you can handle this?" I asked.

"Of course I'm sure," she said. "I won't be driving, just rocking."

She reminded me that she'd raised two boys who'd moved off and raised families of their own.

"I miss having the little ones more than I miss my dear sweet Harry," she admitted sheepishly.

I LOVED WORKING AND LOOKED forward to seeing my customers again, but that week I had a tough time staying focused. In the middle of talking with Iris Weinstein about a two-page spread for the September back-to-school supplement, I started worrying that maybe I hadn't pumped enough milk for Violet.

I wrapped up my presentation in two shakes of a lamb's tail and went home to check on Violet. When I walked in Margaret was easing herself back and forth in the rocking chair, Violet sound asleep in her lap.

I can only guess I had a look of panic on my face because Margaret looked up and asked, "What's wrong?"

"Apparently nothing," I said, laughing at my own foolishness. "I thought maybe—"

Margaret chuckled. "You're a new mama. New mamas worry about everything. But after you've had two or three more—"

I started laughing before she could finish the thought. "I doubt I'll ever—"

"Don't be so sure," she said. "Don't be so sure."

I WENT BACK TO WORK that afternoon, but twice more that week I came home in the middle of the day just to check on Violet. I knew Margaret was taking good care of her, but the truth was I missed her.

AS WEEKS TURNED INTO MONTHS, Violet and I settled into a daily routine. It began before the sun was fully across the horizon. I would lift my sleepy angel from her crib, snuggle her to my breast and cuddle her while she filled her tummy. Before she was two months old she'd begun to smile. Not the sort of smile that can be attributed to baby gas, but a real smile. A smile that lit up her face and made her eyes shine. In those early morning hours I held her and talked to her and told her of all the wonderful things we would one day do.

"Next summer when you're walking we'll go to the park every Saturday," I'd promise. "We'll sit by the pond and feed the ducks..."

Every day there seemed to be a new wonder to marvel at, and I never tired of holding her or carrying on my one-sided conversations.

The days were long and woven tightly together. I spent the mornings and evenings caring for Violet and the days working. There was no longer time for dinner with the girls or a night at the movies. My conversations were limited to specifications for quarter-page ads and double truck spreads or the baby talk promises I made to Violet.

Weekends were used for playing catch up. I did the laundry, ran errands and got ready for the coming week, which was almost always like the one that came before it. On a really good week I might be able to squeeze in a quick visit to the apothecary or a kitchen table lunch with Margaret, and even then I carried Violet strapped to my chest.

THE PARTY

A few days before Violet turned three months old I found Nick's wristwatch. It had dropped down behind the nightstand. I scooped it up and put in in my handbag thinking I would drive by the gas station and drop it off.

That morning I took special care with my makeup and wore the same blue silk dress I'd worn the day we met. I told myself to expect nothing, that if he wanted to come back he would have done so of his own accord. That's what I told myself, but even I didn't believe it.

Being alone all the time was more difficult than I'd imagined it to be. As much as I enjoyed every moment spent with Violet, I missed having someone to talk with. I missed hearing Nick tell about the book he was reading or the joke he heard. I missed the back and forth of a male-female relationship and the comfort of having a companion.

That afternoon I scheduled a meeting with Ridgefield Trust, and on my way there I stopped at the gas station where Nick worked. When I pulled in, Herb, the owner, gave me a big smile and a wave.

"Hi, stranger!" he hollered. "What're you doing in this part of town?"

I got out of the car, crossed the lot and gave him a casual hug.

"Hi yourself," I said. "I found Nick's watch and I thought…is he around?"

For a moment Herb just stood there looking at me strangely. "I thought you knew."

"Knew? Knew what?"

"Nick quit three months ago. Moved back to Baltimore."

"No problem," I said lightheartedly. "The watch isn't all that great. I just figured—"

"Want me to look and see if I've got his address?"

I shook my head. "Don't bother; he's probably forgotten about it anyway."

I got back in my car and drove off.

IT'S STRANGE, BUT KNOWING NICK had left town like that made me stop missing him altogether. It was kind of like a light bulb turned on inside my head, and I could see what a foolish romantic I'd been. Although there had been times when I shied away from believing what Ophelia had said about Nick, I now realized she'd seen what I hadn't.

That afternoon when I left Ridgefield Trust, I drove over to Ophelia's. We sat on the back porch and drank dandelion tea.

"You were right about Nick," I told her. "Seeing as he was Violet's daddy, I didn't want to believe he'd completely turn his back on her. I thought maybe in time…"

Ophelia shook her head. "It's time for you to say goodbye to those troubles and move on to the next batch. Every road has potholes. You can't change that. All you can do is keep going and not let yourself get stuck in them."

As I drove home that day I opened the window of the car and heaved the watch into an overgrown wooded lot.

"So long, Nick!" I shouted and kept on moving.

A WEEK LATER NICOLE CALLED.

"Somebody is turning twenty-five this coming weekend," she teased.

"Good grief," I said. "I've been so busy I haven't given my birthday a thought."

"Maybe you haven't," she replied, "but we have."

I knew "we" meant the girls at the *Tribune*. "Oh, you don't have to—"

"Not another word," she cut in. "This Saturday we're taking you out for a birthday celebration, and don't even think about saying you can't go because of Violet. She'll survive one night with a babysitter."

I laughed; Nicole had read my mind. "Okay, I'll ask Margaret and see if she's available."

"I've already asked," Nicole said, "and she's happy to do it."

We chatted a few minutes longer, and by the time I'd hung up the phone I was looking forward to my night out.

That week I splurged—bought myself a new dress and had my hair done. This was the first time I'd pampered myself in months, and it felt good. Very good. Dressing up and going out to party made me feel like I was shedding the weighty cloak of responsibility. For this one night, I would be Cinderella going to the ball.

I brought Violet and her equipment down to Margaret's where she would spend the night.

"I'll pick her up tomorrow morning," I said, then kissed Violet goodbye and left.

WHEN I ARRIVED AT THE Horsehead Brewery, the party was already in full swing. Not only had Nicole invited the gals from the Classifieds but there were also a bunch of newcomers, people I'd seen around the office but barely knew in passing, and a few other faces that were totally unfamiliar. The music was loud and the laughter even louder. For a moment I felt out of place, but before I could turn and leave Nicole spotted me and hurried over. She grabbed my hand and pulled me back through the crowd.

It started harmlessly enough. I ordered a glass of wine and stood there chatting with the girls from the *Tribune*, showing them pictures of Violet in the little album I carried around.

"She's sitting up now," I said proudly and thumbed through to the page where she was propped between two pillows.

Francine, a plump brunette from the features department, came over and gave me a sloppy hug.

"Forget baby pictures," she said. "There's someone you gotta meet."

Vince was that someone. He was the kind of man I found myself attracted to all too often, one who oozes charm and considers himself prettier than you.

"So, you're the birthday girl," he said. "Well, then, let's get you a drink!"

There are some men who have the kind of sexiness that draws you in; Vince had it in abundance. He flagged the bartender, then turned and looked at me as if I was standing naked.

"Let's see," he mused. "I'm thinking you're the kind of woman who could handle bourbon on the rocks."

He ordered the drink before I had time to say otherwise. It was much too strong for me, and after not drinking for a year I had little tolerance for even a glass of wine. The bartender set the drink in front of me, and I sipped it slowly. When my glass was half-empty, Vince ordered me another.

The Horsehead had a musical trio that night, and as a throaty singer belted out *Baby One More Time* he pulled me onto the dance floor and we gyrated to the beat of the music. I danced as if I was Britney Spears and Vince mouthed the words, "Let me show you how I'll do you..."

I'd tell you more about the party, but there's not a lot I remember. I recall the pulsing beat of *Drop It Like It's Hot* and the burn of bourbon as it slid down my throat. I also remember Vince, his hand strong against my back pulling my body into his as we moved with the music. Most everything else is a blur of music, laughter and passion.

The one thing I still cannot remember is leaving.

I WOKE AT DAWN AS I always did, but before my eyes focused I felt an arm draped across my waist. I knew something was wrong, and a sense of panic rose in my chest. Without moving I opened my eyes and looked around the room. My new dress was lying on the floor in a crumpled heap. Someone else's clothes were scattered about. I heard the sound of traffic on the highway and knew we were in a motel.

I shifted my eyes to the side and saw Vince's face. He was sound asleep with his mouth hanging open. When I eased myself from beneath his arm, he snorted and turned on his other side. I waited until he settled again then climbed from the bed, pulled on my dress and hurried out of the room. I was hoping my car was in the parking lot, but it wasn't. It was back at the Horsehead.

Thank God I had my pocketbook. I pulled out my phone and called for a cab.

My car was right where I'd left it, two blocks north of the Horsehead. I climbed in and drove straight home. The shame I felt was overwhelming.

Never again, I vowed. I hated myself for being weak-willed and vulnerable. How could I, a supposedly intelligent woman, sleep with a man whose face I could barely remember? Whose last name I didn't even know? I reminded myself I was a mother with a baby to raise. I had responsibilities. Over and over again I promised myself I would never again do something so stupid.

MARGARET MUST HAVE HEARD ME when I unlocked the front door. She opened her apartment door and poked her head out.

"I was getting a bit worried," she said. "Are you all right?"

I gave a forced smile and nodded. "I had a few drinks, so I slept at Nicole's rather than drive home."

"Well, that was smart," she said. "I'm glad you girls had a good time."

I had little to say. I felt certain the truth of what I'd done was written on my face in bright red neon letters. I could almost imagine the word "whore" blinking on and off like a stoplight.

AFTER I PUT VIOLET DOWN for her nap, I showered and scrubbed my skin until it was almost raw. Even then I could still feel the slime of the previous night stuck to me. Luckily I kept a supply of breast milk in the refrigerator and freezer. For three days I used that stored milk to feed Violet and poured the bourbon-laced milk I pumped down the drain.

There was no way I was going to let my baby suffer the consequences of what I'd done. I'm a mama, I kept reminding myself. I've got responsibilities.

THE CONSEQUENCES

ama used to say, "Be careful what you wish for because you just might get it." Of course, back then I was wishing for things like curly hair or a boyfriend. But her words came back to haunt me when I missed my period three weeks after the party.

Impossible, I thought. It was a one-night stand. A drunken orgy with a man I'd just met. I reminded myself I wasn't a woman who conceived easily. Ryan and I tried for a year. I timed my cycles as closely as you'd time a roast in the oven, and still we'd met with failure.

My getting pregnant for the second time in a year had about the same odds as winning the lottery, so I fluffed it off and waited another two weeks. Still no period.

Friday afternoon I was on my way to pick up Violet and stopped at the drugstore. Reluctantly I purchased another pregnancy test.

It remained stuck in the side pocket of my purse until late Sunday evening. Once Violet was sleeping and the house so quiet I could hear my heart beat, I carried the kit into the bathroom and sat on the toilet. This time I prayed the strip would not change color. I had my hands full with one baby and couldn't imagine how I'd handle two. But the thought of having a second baby wasn't nearly as frightening as the thought of explaining where it had come from.

The strip turned blue, and I began to sob.

After Baby Girl left my life, I had pleaded with God to send me another baby. Now I would have not one but two. *Be careful what you wish for...*

That night I didn't sleep a wink. I kept thinking about my life, about all the things I'd done wrong, the poor choices I'd made. I also pulled up the few things I'd done right. I'd loved Baby Girl enough to put her happiness ahead of mine. I'd left Ryan and discovered I could make it on my own. I'd chosen Violet over Nick. And now, even in the midst of turmoil and fear, I knew I would love this baby just as I loved Violet.

MY THREE BEST FRIENDS WERE Nicole, Margaret and Ophelia. I needed to talk to someone and I couldn't bring myself to tell Margaret or Ophelia, so I told Nicole.

"No bullshavicky?" she said. As I've said before "bullshavicky" is Nicole's favorite word, and she knows a dozen different ways to use it.

"I didn't even know you were seeing anybody," she added.

"I'm not," I said. "It happened the night of the party."

Her mouth fell open. "Vince?"

I nodded. "Yes, but don't say anything about it because I'm not telling him."

"That is such bullshavicky! You've gotta tell him, it's his kid, make him pay—"

I cut her off. "No! I make enough to support two kids and myself. I don't need him or his money."

"But—"

I shook my head before she even got started. "You're not going to talk me into it. I've had enough of men like that in my life. First Ryan, then Nick. I'm tired of being stupid about relationships. From here on in, it's going to be my family and me. That's it."

"You're bongo crazy." She gave me her raised eyebrow look. "If it was me, I'd make him pay."

Nicole could be rough around the edges, but she was a good friend and when I needed to talk she was always there. She promised to be my birthing partner.

When a woman is pregnant she goes through a lot of changes; not just her body, but her emotional needs change also. Nicole was there for me. Week after week she came to visit, sometimes with a pizza or a container of Chinese take-out, sometimes with a movie we could sit and watch while Violet snuggled at my breast.

I DREADED THE DAY I would have to tell Margaret and Ophelia. They were not like Nicole; they were older and lived more respectable lives. Ophelia had no children, and Margaret's first boy had been born a year after she'd married Henry. I imagined they'd view one baby out of wedlock as a permissible lapse in judgment, but two babies might make me seem to have little or no morals.

By the beginning of January my waist had grown thick, and it was obvious that I'd added some weight. I couldn't put it off any longer. I telephoned Ophelia and said I'd like to take her and Margaret to lunch.

"I'd much rather you come here," she said. "It's too cold for the porch but the kitchen is toasty warm, and I'm anxious to try my new recipe for chicken fricassee."

"Only if you promise to make dandelion tea," I replied.

She laughed and said she'd have the tea and ginger cookies as well.

THAT SATURDAY WITH VIOLET SAFELY buckled into her car seat and Margaret riding up front with me, we headed for Ophelia's house.

Keeping such a secret from a friend is more difficult than you might think. You watch every word that comes from your mouth. You wonder, if I say this thing or that thing, am I giving myself away? The easiness of your friendship becomes strained, and before long they start to wonder if perchance they've done something to offend you.

Margaret and I rode in silence most of the way. Once or twice she started to say something, then turned it off as if it were a thought not worth pursuing.

When we turned onto Haber Street she gave a deep sigh.

"It'll be good to see Ophelia again," she said.

"Yes," I replied. "It will."

I WAITED UNTIL WE HAD finished our lunch, and then as we were having our tea and cookies I told them I was expecting another baby.

Margaret sat with her jaw hanging open for a moment. Finally she sighed. "Oh, dear."

Ophelia smiled. "I know. Are you due in May or June?"

"Um... May," I answered. "But how—"

"You've got the glow," she said. "I noticed it the last time you were here."

"Now I get it!" Margaret chimed in. "This is why you've been so close-mouthed." She gave a grin. "Thank goodness! I've been worried sick you were going to move out and leave me."

The funny thing about that afternoon is that neither of them asked who the father was. They asked how I felt and if I knew whether I was having a boy or girl. They also asked if there was something they could do to help out, but neither of them turned up their noses or looked at me with a disparaging glare.

I thought about how my own mama had slammed the receiver down in my ear when she heard the news and was reminded of something Daddy once told me.

"God doesn't always give you what you want," he said, "but he always gives you what you need."

I had everything I needed. Good friends and a family I could call my own. That night after I tucked Violet into her crib, I said a prayer and thanked God for giving me what I needed instead of all the other things I'd been wishing for.

A Family Of Three

Felix arrived two weeks early as a middle-of-the-night baby. Wearing her nightgown and robe, Margaret scurried up the stairs to stay with Violet while Nicole whisked me off to the Sisters of Mercy. By the time we got to the hospital, I was well into labor and went straight to the delivery room. He was born within the hour.

Two days later I was home with two babies. By then Violet was walking, had started to say a few words and graduated to whole milk. Felix was now the baby at my breast. With two cribs and toys scattered about, the little room was crowded but manageable.

For the second time in just over a year, I was out on maternity leave. It was during the last week before returning to work that I began thinking I should tell Vince he was a father. As far as I was concerned I would have been happy to leave things as they were, but I worried about Felix. I imagined him as a young man asking why I'd never even told his father about him.

"Were you ashamed of me, Mama?" he might ask. Of course I would answer no, but still I would have no excuse to give.

I thought about this for three days; then I called Amy Elkins. Months earlier Nicole had mentioned that Vince was Amy's friend.

"Vince, the fellow who was at the Horsehead party last September," I said. "I'd like to get in touch with him; do you have his last name and phone number?"

She did and gave it to me.

I let another day go by before I finally called him.

On the Thursday before I was to return to work, I waited until both babies were sleeping; then I went into the living room and dialed his number. He answered on the first ring.

"Hi," I said. "This is Cheryl Ann."

There were a few moments of silence; then he said, "Do I know you?"

I could feel the lump rising into my throat. "Last September, the party at the Horsehead, you and I..."

Again there was silence.

"The motel on Route 23..."

"Oh, geez," he said, laughing. "Yeah, I remember. How are you?"

"Good," I said. "Real good. But I think there's something you should know."

He waited but said nothing.

"I had a baby," I finally blurted out.

"Oh, shit! I hope you're not trying to say it's mine, because there's no way in hell—"

Before he could continue I said, "It is yours. I'm sure because you're the only one I've been with."

"I don't know what kind of game you're playing, but I'm not falling for it. That kid isn't mine, and I'm not giving you a dime! If you're looking for—"

"I don't want your money," I said. "I make enough to support my family. But I thought since you're Felix's father you might want to be involved in his life."

"No, I don't!" he said and slammed the receiver down.

For a moment I sat there too stunned to speak. Then I began to cry. I cried not for me but for Felix and perhaps for my own daddy, the man Felix had been named after. It was a painful thing to be without a daddy. It left a hole in your life.

A short while later I heard Felix starting to whimper and I wondered if on some plane of consciousness, an understanding far beyond that of mortals, he'd grasped the words his father said.

I lifted him from his crib, carried him to the living room and held him to my breast. Hours later as he lay sleeping in my arms I swore that neither of my children would pay for my mistakes. I would see to it that they had a good life, even if it was without a daddy.

THE DAYS TURNED INTO WEEKS and the weeks into years. The spring Violet turned three and Felix celebrated his second birthday, Margaret set up a birthday party in the backyard. It was only our little group and a handful of friends, but she decorated with balloons and had party hats for everyone. We laughed and played games all afternoon. Auntie Nicole gave Felix a hobby horse with wheels and Violet a tricycle. That afternoon she took pictures of the kids and me.

Those pictures were almost magical. I could actually see the happiness in their faces. I chose a shot where Felix had a piece of cake stuck to his cheek, had it blown up to poster size and hung it on the living room wall as a reminder of the family we'd grown into.

During those years I did very little socializing. Once in a while I'd have Margaret stay with the babies so I could have dinner with Nicole or the girls from the *Tribune*. But those instances were few and far between.

Somehow I had evolved into something that could only be

described as neither fish nor fowl. I was single but had little in common with my single friends. I had plenty in common with other mothers but I was the sole provider, so when they did playdates or mom get-togethers I was out calling on customers. Evenings were spent at home because people seldom invited a single woman to tag along or be a dinner guest unless it was a fix-up. A blind date. *No, thanks.*

I'D BE LYING IF I said there weren't times when I longed to feel a man's arms around me, to feel the warmth of his body next to mine or be touched in the way that only a lover touches you. In the last hours of the evening when my babies were asleep and I sat alone on the sofa, a romantic movie would remind me of those things and a feeling of loneliness would come upon me. When that happened I would go into the nursery and watch my babies sleep.

God gives you what you need, not what you want.

I had exactly what I needed, a family where I could love and be loved.

THE HOUSE

I have heard it said that the love of a child can inspire you to do things far greater than you might otherwise have done, and I believe it's true. I spent my childhood years on a street where making do was the best you could hope for, and I grew up believing I deserved nothing more than what I had. When life ran roughshod over me I accepted that as my lot. Then my children came along. That changed everything.

I had two small lives entrusted to my care, and I wanted it to be better for them than it had been for me. I allowed them to experience all the things I hadn't. I said it was okay to build a Lincoln log fort in the middle of the living room or have a lineup of baby dolls sitting on the sofa. People were more important than things, and caring trumped neatness. These are the things I tried to teach the children. I wanted them to understand what it meant to love and be loved

But as they grew, so did the size and number of toys. They filled the small bedroom and spilled out into the hall. On any given day you could find scooters, blocks and balls strewn from one end of the apartment to the other. We were rapidly outgrowing our space.

For Violet's fifth birthday, Margaret gave her a grown-up bike with training wheels and that seemed to be the thing that pushed us over the edge.

"I think we need to find a larger apartment," I told Margaret.

"I never thought I'd say this," she replied, "but I think you're right."

FOR ALMOST A MONTH I searched for a three-bedroom apartment fairly close to where we were. The nursery school was nearby, I had an easy commute to work and Margaret was always willing to babysit. The problem I ran into was that we didn't live in an apartment building area. Cape cods, ranches and two-story houses lined every street this side of town.

On an afternoon when I was weary from looking at apartments smaller than what we had, the kids and I met Auntie Nicole for lunch at McDonalds. While the kids explored the playground, Nicole and I sat and talked.

"This search for an apartment is turning into a nightmare," I said. "I haven't seen one any bigger than what we've got."

Nicole stuffed an extra-long French fry into her mouth and said around it, "Apartment bullshavicky, what you need is a house."

"A house?" I laughed in disbelief. "What makes you think I can afford a house?"

"What makes you think you can't?" she answered.

I thought about that question for a moment and then admitted I didn't have an answer. I guess it was one of those things I thought I wasn't entitled to.

That evening, after both kids were asleep, I sat down with my checkbook, the last two years' income statements and a list of monthly expenses. I looked at the average home cost in the area, figured the mortgage payment, added insurance and allowed for a small margin of repairs. Much to my surprise, I discovered I could do it if the cost of the house was $85,000 or under. Preferably under. I gathered up the newspaper real estate sections where I'd been searching under "Rental Apartments" and turned to the page that listed homes for sale.

For well over a month I looked at homes that were smaller than an apartment. Or drastically in need of repair. Or somewhere in the middle of nowhere. Or butting up against a highway. Then I saw an ad for a three-bedroom ranch. It didn't list the price but offered a deep discount for a quick sale and gave a phone number for Cindy Callahan of Morris and Morris.

I called and she said the house was listed at $109,900.

"But," she added in a whispery voice, "I know for a fact the owner is being transferred and anxious to get moving. If you offered ninety-nine, I think he'd take it."

I explained that was higher than I could afford to go.

"I'm looking for something in the seventy-to-eighty thousand range," I said.

Cindy said she had a few houses in that general price range, and we made a date for Saturday.

The prospect of moving to a house excited the kids almost as much as it did me, so they were full of questions when we got to the real estate office. The minute I sat down at the desk, Felix gave Cindy his million-dollar smile and said, "I'm five; can I have my own room?"

"You're not five," Violet argued, "you're four. I'm five!"

"Cute kids," Cindy said. "Your little guy reminds me of my nephew." She turned her computer around and showed me the picture on the screen. "See. That's Elgin; don't they look alike?"

I didn't see that much of a resemblance but nodded nonetheless. "You said you had a few houses in the seventy-to-eighty thousand range?"

"I do," she replied, "but they're basically dumps."

She pulled up a few pictures and showed them to me. When a

halfway decent cape cod came on screen she shook her head and said, "Sewer problems. Backs up all the time."

"Oh, too bad," I replied, and she moved on to the next one.

We looked at five pictures, and there wasn't one house that looked inviting. A house with the front porch leaning to one side needed work. More work than I could afford.

"It's really tough to find something decent in that price range," Cindy said. "If you can go up to ninety-five or maybe ninety-nine, I've got a nice cape cod on Hillmoor. And you know about that really sweet ranch on Prescott. The owners of the ranch are very anxious to sell, and I know they'd be willing to talk deal."

If I hadn't already looked at more ugly houses than I could count, I might have turned away from such a suggestion. Instead I shrugged and said I'd be willing to take a look at it.

Of course, one look was all I needed. I fell in love with the house. More importantly so did the kids. As Cindy and I stood in the kitchen talking price and bargaining possibilities, I looked out into the backyard and saw the kids playing on a swing set. It was one of those moments that grabs hold of your heart and refuses to let go.

That night I refigured my budget six ways from Sunday, and the absolute most I could swing was $87,000. I wrote a letter to the owners and e-mailed it to Cindy to pass along with my offer. In the letter I explained how we had all three fallen in love with the house and although I knew it was worth what they were asking, I was a single mom and this was all I could afford.

"I can see the love that's gone into your house," I wrote, "and if we are fortunate enough to get it, I promise to treasure and care for it just as you have."

I hit Send and started to pray.

Three days later Cindy called.

"They accepted your offer," she said.

A FOREVER PLACE

On moving day the two burly men from Budget Moving carried out seventy-six cartons plus all the furniture we'd accumulated over the years. Once the truck pulled out of the driveway, I loaded the kids into the car and turned back to give Margaret one last hug.

"This isn't goodbye," I told her.

"I know," she said sadly. "But you'll be a half a mile away, and that's not the same as having you upstairs."

I knew what she said was true and hugged her all the more tightly. "We'll be back to visit every weekend. I promise."

She gave a tight little smile. "Anytime you need a babysitter..."

"You'll be the first one I call."

We gave each other one last hug, and I climbed into the car.

"Take care of yourself," she said, "and remember if you need anything..."

"We'll be fine." I waved one last goodbye and backed out of the driveway.

THE FIRST DAY IN OUR house was bedlam. We focused on getting things set up for our most immediate needs. Dishes in the cabinet, sheets on the beds, toothbrushes and pajamas unpacked. It was almost nine when Violet and Felix crawled into bed, happy and exhausted.

Later that evening when everything was so quiet I could hear the crickets in the backyard chirping, I walked through the house looking at every room, noticing every small detail: the moldings, the brick fireplace, the built-in bookcase in the living room. I ran my hand along the shelves and imagined them one day filled with books, pictures and the memorabilia we'd collected in the years of our life.

There is no way to explain the pride I felt at that moment. My heart was filled to overflowing, and as I stood there looking into the future a tear slid down my face. It wasn't sadness but an overwhelming feeling that everything was better than I ever imagined it could be. I had the family I'd always wanted, and now we even had our very own home.

I thought back to my days on Spruce Street and how Mama had said if I didn't find myself a man and settle down I was never going to amount to a hill of beans.

You were wrong, Mama. Look at what I've done. I have a fine family and a lovely little house, and I've done it all by myself. Without a man in my life.

THE FIRST TWO WEEKS WE were in the house I was on vacation. I couldn't imagine a vacation better than cleaning every little corner and putting each piece of our life in precisely the right spot. Violet is a bit like me. Before the second day was done, she had emptied out all of her cartons and arranged her room exactly as she wanted it. Baby dolls sat along the windowsill, a dollhouse against the back wall and her little table and chairs set in the spot where sun dappled the carpet.

Felix was the opposite. He opened the cartons, took out the dump truck he wanted and left the rest to be unpacked another time.

THE FURNITURE WE'D BROUGHT WITH us was okay, but it wasn't enough. The house was quite a bit larger than the apartment, so the dining room sat empty and we needed a dresser for Felix's room. We also needed a few more lamps and some nightstands. On our fourth day in the new house, the kids and I headed for the Salvation Army Thrift shop.

I was hoping to see the sweet woman who had taken me under her wing years earlier when I came with Ryan, but this time an elderly man was behind the counter. I had no name and only a vague description of the woman.

"She had silver hair, on the short side, a pleasant smile," I said. "You know of anyone like that?"

He gave a shrug and shook his head. "A description like that fits most of the volunteers who work here. Now if you had a name..."

"No problem." I thanked him for his time and moved on.

We spent the afternoon wandering through aisles piled high with furniture of every shape, size and color. I selected a rectangular-shaped dining room table with a badly scratched top, four matching chairs and two that didn't match but were close enough. Felix was supposed to pick out a dresser for his room, but instead he chose a toy box. In the end I added a dresser because regardless of preference, he needed a place to put his clothes. I also added three lamps and two nightstands that needed to be sanded and refinished.

The following day the Salvation Army truck pulled into our driveway and delivered everything.

I spent the next five days doing countless runs to Home Depot as I sanded and refinished the tabletop and nightstands. Long after the kids had gone to bed, I'd still be sanding and polishing. It might sound like a lot of work, but it didn't feel that way. I suppose because it truly was a labor of love.

By the end of the second week, everything was unpacked and put away. We were ready for company, so I invited Nicole, Ophelia and Margaret to dinner.

Each of them came with gifts to celebrate the new house. Margaret gave us a box filled with fluffy white towels. Nicole brought a wrought iron wine rack and six bottles of wine.

"Wine?" I chuckled. "You're incorrigible."

"No bullshavicky?" Nicole said with a laugh. "But now that you've got your own house, I thought you'd be doing some male entertaining."

Although I doubted it, I smiled at the thought.

Ophelia was the last to hand me her gift. It was a crystal bowl filled with potpourri.

"This is my special mix," she said. "You'll always know what someone is thinking because the potpourri reflects their thoughts in the fragrance."

I liked that idea. "Will it work for kids also?"

She gave a clever little smile and nodded.

THAT EVENING WE GATHERED AROUND my newly-refinished dining room table and ate the homemade lasagna I'd pulled from the oven. We talked, laughed and told stories. For the first time ever, I could see the rest of my life stretched out in front me: years of happiness sitting here at this table, sharing pieces of life with my little family and our friends.

As I set out a pot of coffee and a plate of chocolate chip cookies, I knew nothing would ever be more perfect than what I had right now.

"The kids and I all love this house," I said. "We're planning to live here forever."

"Forever is a very long time," Ophelia replied. "You never know what changes life will bring."

There is a saying that goes something like this: People come into your life for a reason, a season or a lifetime. It was my belief that I had already passed through all of those who were there for a reason or season. I had the family and friends who were there for a lifetime, and I needed nothing more.

I remember how I chuckled at the thought of changes and said I was certain that this was my forever.

THE FAVOR

Over the course of our first winter in the house I didn't give a thought to differing possibilities of forever. I was too busy being happy with the here and now. In the fall Violet started kindergarten, Felix went into pre-K and the *Tribune* promoted me to district manager, which increased my income considerably and gave us money for a few added luxuries. From time to time we could now have a night out with dinner, a movie and hot chocolate afterward.

The days fairly flew by that winter. It was Thanksgiving then Christmas, and for the first time ever we had a real Christmas tree. The house was filled with the fragrance of pine and cookies fresh from the oven. The kids and I baked hundreds of Christmas cookies, topped them with red sugar sprinkles and boxed them to give to friends and neighbors. It was a season of good will such as I'd never known.

On Christmas Eve Violet and Felix napped in the afternoon, so they got to stay up and go to evening church service with me. The three of us sat in the first pew and sang in voices that resonated with happiness. That evening I gave both Violet and Felix a present to open. These were the two gifts I'd worked on in the evenings when the house was quiet and the children sleeping.

They were hand painted nameplates for their bedroom door. Violet's name was written out in swirling script and decorated with flowers. Felix's was done in block letters shaped to resemble a train.

Santa would bring the toys while they slept, but I wanted them to understand this gift was from me. It was my way of telling each of them they deserved and now had a place of their own.

⁂

TO ME, OPHELIA WAS A mother, sister and best friend all rolled into one. Ever since that first day when I walked into the apothecary looking to buy a box of dandelion tea, she was there for me. In good times she laughed with me, in bad times she let me lean on her shoulder. In the darkest days when I knew I would have to give up Baby Girl, Ophelia was there. She encouraged me to move from one day to the next, held my hand and told me somewhere beyond my sorrow I would find happiness.

Until my dying day there is nothing Ophelia could ask of me that I would not do for her. But this time I was sorely tempted to say no. I alluded to it, but the bottom line was I simply couldn't flat out refuse.

She began by telling me about the young man who for the past three years came every spring and turned the soil for her garden.

"It's a big job," she said, "and I could never do it myself." She explained he dug up the weeds, cleared the overgrowth and plowed the ground into furrows.

"All that work, and he won't take a nickel in payment; claims it's just a neighborly kindness," she added.

"That certainly is nice of him," I said and moved on to try to talk of what she'd be growing this season.

Ophelia apparently wasn't ready to talk about the garden; instead she wanted to talk about William McLeod.

"A nice young man like him ought to have a girlfriend or wife maybe." She sat back in her chair, took a sip of her tea, then said, "Someone like you would be perfect for him."

"Oh, I don't think—"

"He might be a year or so older than you, but nice looking."

"I haven't had very good experiences with men, and I really don't—"

"Those weren't men," she said sharply. "They were overgrown boys with no sense of responsibility. Now William, he's different."

"He sounds like a lovely person, but I'm happy with the way my life is and—"

Ignoring my objections, she continued. "I mentioned you to William, and he said he'd like to give you a call if you wouldn't mind."

Although the thought of a gentleman caller did have a certain amount of appeal, the kids were my main concern and we didn't need a man complicating our now peaceful existence. "I'd rather—"

I think Ophelia knew what I was about to say, and she interrupted before I could get there.

"I'd consider it a personal favor," she said.

That request trumped any further objections I had. I sighed. "Okay."

THE NEXT DAY I RECEIVED a text from William. "Hi Cheryl Ann. Ophelia Browne gave me your number and suggested I call. Would you mind if I did?"

His message was not the least bit flowery; it was just straightforward and sincere. I liked that. I texted him back and said I would enjoy hearing from him. The thought of a dinner date in a place that didn't have a clown or a person making animals out of balloons suddenly had some appeal.

He sent another text asking if eight o'clock the next evening would be a good time to call. I texted back that it would be.

He sent a third text saying he'd look forward to it.

HE CALLED AT EXACTLY EIGHT, and for a minute or two there was a touch of that "blind date" awkwardness. He started off by reminding me that he was William McLeod, Ophelia's friend.

"Yes, she speaks very highly of you," I said.

His voice was warm and friendly, but he sounded a bit nervous.

"I've looked forward to talking to you," he said.

Once the conversation got going, I found he was extremely interesting. He told me about the farm he'd bought three years earlier.

"I was an accountant before that," he explained, "but my heart wasn't in it. My grandparents lived on a farm for most of their life, and I spent summers with them. Dairy farming is what I've always wanted to do, so when this place came up for sale I grabbed it. 'Course there's more than cows here," he said and told me of the crops he grew.

Instead of him just coming out and asking for a date, we chatted like two old friends catching up after years apart. We talked about how long each of us had known Ophelia, what music we liked, what movies we'd seen.

Given my previous experiences, I figured it was better to warn him up front.

"I have two children," I said.

"That's wonderful," he replied and asked how old they were.

I liked that he didn't just gloss over their existence but wanted to know more about them. When I told him a few stories about Violet and Felix, he listened attentively and gave a chuckle in all the right places. After we'd talked for almost forty minutes he said if I had no objection, he'd like to call again.

I had no objection.

Starting Date

William and I spoke three times before the Tuesday when he asked if he could take me to dinner.

"Saturday evening?" he said.

"I'd like that," I answered.

By then we had already crossed two hurdles. I knew he was an interesting conversationalist, and he had no problem with my having children. It was a good start, but it had been more than five years since I'd last been out on a date and a new kind of insecurity began to pick at me.

I started to worry about my appearance, silly stuff I normally didn't give a second thought: my hair, my weight, what to wear, what not to wear. The actual problem was none of those things. The real problem was I had lost whatever dating confidence I once had.

What if he saw me and decided I wasn't his type? What then? Would he whip out a cell phone and say he had to rush off because of a sudden emergency?

Now I can laugh at how foolish all of this sounds, but back then it was very real and very intimidating.

Rather than face the prospect of rejection, I tapped out another text. This time I attached my picture.

"Just so you know what to expect," I wrote. "Hope you are not disappointed." I hesitated a moment, took a deep breath and then clicked Send.

Thirty seconds later I got my answer.

"Wow! Now I am REALLY looking forward to meeting you."

When I saw "really" in capital letters, I breathed a sigh of relief.

AS I GOT DRESSED THAT Saturday you could have easily believed I was dining with Brad Pitt or George Clooney. I tried on a dozen different outfits. First it was a red dress with high-heeled pumps—wrong on both counts. Too much cleavage and the shoes felt wobbly. Then I tried on a few of the suits I'd worn for business. Too severe looking. Three of the four pant outfits I tried made me feel fat. Finally I settled on a pair of black pants and an aqua sweater that brought out the blue-green color of my eyes.

Our date was set for seven-thirty but by seven I was dressed, had the kids in their jammies and had given the babysitter her last-minute instructions. At seven-fifteen the doorbell rang.

He's as anxious as I am, I thought.

I opened the door, and for a moment we stood there just looking at one another.

He spoke first.

"Hi, Cheryl Ann," he said and stuck out his hand to shake mine. "I've been looking forward to meeting you." The crooked little turned-up smile he gave me said I'd chosen the right outfit.

I turned, called back that I was leaving and scooted out the door. It was much too soon for him to meet Violet and Felix.

SOMETIMES MAGIC HAPPENS. NOT BECAUSE a guy is the handsomest man in the room or because the girl is the most beautiful, but because when they look into each other's eyes they see what's inside and realize this is the person they've been waiting for.

That's how it was that night. William wasn't the kind of guy a woman turns to look at, but he was by far the most interesting man I'd ever dated. That evening we drank red wine and talked just as we had on the telephone. Our conversation was both intimate and open. Whatever blind-date anxiety we initially had was long gone.

When I mentioned the children, he leaned in with his eyes fixed on my face.

"Do they have your beautiful blue eyes?" he asked.

"Well, their eyes are blue," I answered, but I felt the color rising in my cheeks.

ONCE WHEN I WAS GOING through a rough time and questioning whether I would ever again love or be loved, I asked Ophelia what made her fall in love with Edward.

"How can you not love a man who looks at you so adoringly?" she answered.

That's exactly how I felt on my first date with William. When he leaned across the table, I looked into the soft brown of his eyes and saw something I had never before seen. It was a look that promised sincerity.

AFTER THAT FIRST DATE, WE saw each other regularly; two, three, sometimes four times a week. Often we spent the evening in my living room with the kids. Felix and Violet were both enthralled with William's stories of living on a farm.

The third time he came to spend the evening with us, William brought both kids a book about farm life.

Felix's book was titled *Daddy Drives A Tractor*. He leafed through the pages then handed the book to William and asked him to read it.

"Sure." William tugged Felix up onto the sofa beside him. "I live on a farm," he began, "and my daddy drives a tractor. A big red tractor..." Page by page he went through the book, raising and lowering his voice in all the right places. After he'd closed the book, he asked Felix if he'd ever ridden on a tractor.

Felix answered with a wide-eyed shake of his head. "I never even saw a real tractor."

For a few moments William sat there rubbing his chin as if he was giving the situation some serious thought; then he said, "If your mama says it's okay, maybe I could arrange for you to take a ride on my tractor."

Felix looked across to me. "Please, Mama," he begged, "say it's okay for me to ride on the tractor."

I laughed and said yes, when the weather got a bit warmer we would visit the farm and he could go for a ride on the tractor.

Felix and William both grinned; then Violet asked if she could go too.

William nodded. "As long as it's okay with your mama." He turned back to Felix. "Now, are you really, really sure you can hold on tight enough so you won't bounce off when we go up and down hills?"

Felix nodded in wide-eyed wonder. "I'm really sure."

"Well, then, I suppose..."

The funny thing is we were acting like a family long before there was any mention of being one. During the week, when William visited, we stayed in and he spent as much time talking to the kids as he did me. At eight-thirty I'd shuffle them off to bed, and by nine he'd be getting ready to leave.

"Farming is an early-morning business," he'd say and then take me in his arms and kiss me goodnight.

IT WAS THAT WAY FOR almost three months. Then one night he stayed long after the kids had said their prayers and gone to sleep. We sat on the sofa and laughed our way through *Two and a Half Men* then did the same with *Mike and Molly*. When *Hawaii Five-O* came on, William suggested we turn the TV off.

I could tell by the edginess in his voice something was troubling his mind. I clicked the remote and waited. With the sound of the television now gone, he took me in his arms and kissed me more passionately than ever before.

"I can't continue doing this, Cheryl Ann," he said. "It's too painful to come here, be with you and the kids, and then go home to an empty house. I need more."

He again covered my mouth with his. I could feel the strength of his hand against my back as he pulled me closer and held me. The feel of his body against mine aroused passions I wanted to believe forgotten.

Being with William was satisfying and wholesome. I didn't want it to turn into the kind of relationships I'd had before.

"Don't...," I mumbled without any conviction.

"It's too late for that," he said. "I'm already in love with you."

"That doesn't mean—" I can't swear to what I intended to say, but whatever it was he didn't give me time to finish it.

He slid his hand into his pocket, pulled out a small velvet box, thumbed it open and offered it to me. Inside was a diamond solitaire.

"Marry me," he said. "I realize you and the kids are happy living here in this house, but I'll make you happier. I swear I will. I love you with all my heart. I knew from the start we were meant to be together; it's right for me, for you and for the kids."

My heart was screaming, "Yes, yes, yes!", but my brain reminded me of all the mistakes that had come before William.

"I need time," I said.

"Time? For what?" he stammered. "I love you, and I can tell you feel the same about me."

"I do," I said, "but marriage is a big step. I have this house and the kids to think about." I gave feeble reasons instead of telling him why I was so frightened at the thought of marriage.

"Don't use the kids as an excuse," he said. "They'd love living on the farm, and you know it. They'd have room to run and play, have all the pets they want…"

He had a million reasons for why I should marry him, and I had only one reason not to. We talked about it until after midnight, and when he finally started home he handed me the box with the ring.

"I want you to hold on to this while you're thinking things over," he said. "Let it be a reminder of how much I love you."

That was the only time he ever walked away without giving me one last kiss.

No Mistakes

There are moments in life you want to hold on to forever. There are also times you'd like to forget, push to the back of your thoughts and pretend they never happened. The problem is you don't get to make the choice. Your mind takes you back to wherever it wants to go, good or bad. There are weeks, months, years even that I'd like to forget, but they continue to haunt me. They remind me of my mistakes and make me fearful of stumbling down that road again.

It was one thing to have my poor choices bring heartache upon me, but as a mother I couldn't allow it to affect my children. As much as I wanted to be with William I kept asking myself, What if a year or two from now he tires of us? What if like Ryan he finds someone else more pleasing, or like Nick decides he doesn't want the responsibility of children? What then?

Having the house had given me the kind of security I never thought possible. Yes, I loved William, and had it been only me I would have thrown caution to the wind in a heartbeat, but it wasn't only me. I had two kids to think about. Was it fair to risk their security and tender little hearts when another disastrous ending could be just around the corner?

AFTER A SLEEPLESS NIGHT I knew I needed the advice of someone older, wiser and more understanding of life. Who better than Ophelia? She knew both William and me. I telephoned her and asked if she had time to talk.

Less than an hour later Violet and Felix were off wading in the pond, and I was sitting across from Ophelia in one of the wicker chairs in her backyard. I told her of William's proposal and explained that I was undecided.

She looked at me with a bewildered expression. "You don't love him?"

"It's not that," I replied. "I do love him, but I'm afraid of what might happen."

Ophelia said nothing and waited for me to continue.

"When I gave up Baby Girl I trusted Ryan would love me forever, but he didn't. He fell in love with someone else and asked for a divorce. It took me a year to get over him. A year of living like a squatter on that boat, a year of being miserable and filled with hate. When I finally did get my life back together, I met Nick and trusted him. He swore up and down he loved me, but once Violet came along he walked out on us both."

"Do you think William is like either of those men?"

I shook my head. "No, but now the stakes are a lot higher. Back then it was only me; now I've got a house and two kids. They're already fond of William, and if he left us now we'd survive. Yes, there would be a hole in our life, but we'd still have a house to live in and we could go from day to day just as we have been. What if something like that happened after we moved out to the farm—in a year or two or three..."

The possibilities overwhelmed me, and my eyes filled with tears. "I've made so many mistakes, and now..."

Ophelia reached across and took my hand in hers. "Maybe

they weren't all mistakes. Maybe they were God's way of teaching you what life is all about."

One by one Ophelia went through all of my disastrous relationships.

"You were little more than a child when you left home with Ryan," she said. "Not yet a woman capable of understanding life. You made a selfless decision in giving up Baby Girl and in doing so learned what it means to love a child." She gave a saddened sigh and added, "Living through such a loss causes a woman to love more deeply."

She hesitated as her hand gave mine a comforting squeeze. "Then there was your handsome Nick Lombardi. He spoke the truth right from the start, but you didn't listen. He was never meant to be your lifetime partner, yet he gave you Violet. Do you think such a beautiful child can be a mistake?"

I shook my head. "Never," I said, recalling how the moment I first held her in my arms my heart filled with love.

Ophelia lowered her eyes and continued. "And then there was that one-night stand, which was definitely a lesson to be learned. But would you change things and give up having Felix in your life?"

I thought of my son's bright smile and eagerness to learn and again shook my head.

"Think about it," she said softly. "If you hadn't trusted the instincts of your heart, you wouldn't have had either of those wonderful children."

I didn't have to think about it; I knew Ophelia was right. Although my life had not followed the pathway I'd envisioned, I wouldn't have changed anything. Not even Baby Girl. Yes, I still missed her and thought of her often, but I knew she was loved and had given the Stuarts a great deal of happiness.

Somehow in looking back I came to realize my life wasn't nearly as disastrous as I had imagined it to be.

"Thank you," I said, then wrapped my arms around her neck and held my cheek against hers.

THAT EVENING WHEN WILLIAM ARRIVED, the ring he'd given me was on the third finger of my left hand. He noticed it right away.

After a quick glance at my hand, he looked at me with a smile stretched across the full width of his face.

"Does this mean…" he asked.

Words were unnecessary. I nodded, and he saw the answer in my eyes.

He pulled me into his arms and covered my mouth with his. It was a kiss that was both passionate and sweet.

"I swear you will never regret this," he whispered. "I'll love Violet and Felix as if they were my own, and I'll make you the most cherished woman on earth."

This time I did trust. His was a promise that would forever hold true.

THE FOLLOWING SATURDAY WE TOOK the kids out for pizza and asked how they would feel about living on a farm.

"We'd have to sell our house and move there," I explained. "Mister McLeod's farm is in Burnsville. That's where Aunt Ophelia lives."

Felix bought into the idea immediately. "Will I get to ride on the tractor? And pet the cows?"

"I'm afraid cows don't like to be petted," William answered. "But I've got a whole litter of baby kittens who love to be petted. Plus, you can ride on the tractor any old time you want to."

"Oh, boy!" Felix gave a wide grin and asked if we could move there tomorrow.

"Not tomorrow," I said, "but soon."

I turned to Violet and asked for her thoughts.

She's my little worrier, and true to form she had her brows pinched together.

"What about school?" she asked. "What about leaving Auntie Nicole and Aunt Margaret?"

"There's a really nice school in Burnsville," William said. "And you'd get to ride on the school bus with all the other kids."

"You wouldn't be leaving Auntie Nicole and Aunt Margaret," I added. "We'd go visit them just the same as we go visit Aunt Ophelia now."

Violet's expression remained the same. "Would Felix and I each have our own room?"

"Absolutely!" William said. "And I was thinking maybe you'd like one of those fancy canopy beds."

"Really?"

William nodded. "Really."

"If you marry Mama and we come to live in your farmhouse, does that mean you'll be our daddy?"

William answered her question with one of his own. "It depends. Do you think you and Felix would like to have me as your daddy?"

"Unh-huh." Violet nodded, and her face broke into a smile.

"Well, then, I'd be honored."

OVER THE NEXT FEW MONTHS each day brought some new pleasure, something more to look forward to, something else to be excited about. We visited William's farm countless times; Felix got to ride on the tractor, ride a horse and name all five of the new kittens. They also saw the bedrooms that would soon be theirs, and one Saturday we all went shopping in Burnsville and Violet got to pick out the canopy bed she'd been dreaming about.

As for me, I fell more in love with William with each day that passed. As Ophelia once said, how can you not love a man who adores you and both of your children?

A NEW LIFE

We were married on the first Sunday of November. The ceremony took place in Burnsville at the Good Shepherd Church, a small white clapboard building distinguished only by the steeple that rose above the red and gold of the treetops.

It was a simple service with just a handful of friends and family in attendance. I was hoping Mama would come, but she didn't. She sent a card and said her arthritis was acting up, so she wasn't able to make the trip. Ophelia, who is almost like a mother to me, was there, as was Margaret. Nicole served as my maid of honor and she wore an ivory colored dress, the same as me.

Both kids took part in the ceremony. William had insisted on it.

"I want them to know I'm marrying them along with their mama," he'd said.

Felix was the ring bearer and Violet a flower girl. She looked like a little angel carrying the basket of yellow and white chrysanthemums clipped from Ophelia's garden.

William's brother, Matthew, was his best man, and his parents looked on proudly from the first pew. The only other guests were four couples, farm families from the area and friends of William.

It was the first time I'd met Leroy and Wilma, William's parents, and I liked them right from the start. Leroy was tall and settled looking like William, and Wilma had a sweetness about her that's almost impossible to describe. After the ceremony she kissed William on the cheek then did the same with me. She then pulled the two of us into one giant hug and whispered that if either of the kids or us ever needed anything to call on her.

"We're family," she said, and that thought nestled into my heart like a dish of sweet pudding.

Following the service, we celebrated with coffee and cake in Good Shepherd's Community Room then everyone went home and we came back to the farm. It was fall harvest season, which made it impossible for William to take time for a honeymoon. I was floating on a cloud of happiness, so the part about the honeymoon didn't trouble me at all. In fact, I couldn't think of a place I'd rather be than right there in my forever home with my forever family.

AFTER THE WEDDING I TOOK a week of vacation time and used it to settle into my new life. We'd carted over almost one hundred boxes from what was now called the old house, so I spent the entire week combining "my stuff" and "his stuff" into "our stuff." Of course we ended up with more frying pans, coffee pots and toaster ovens than we could possibly use, so I loaded the car and took the extras to the Sisters of Mercy Thrift Shop.

The next week I returned to work. For as long as I can remember, I've always worked so I had no reason to believe now it would be any different. Monday through Friday I woke the kids, got them dressed and fed, then backed out of the driveway and headed for Wyattsville. Truth be told, though, I missed being there when they climbed off the school bus and when William came in for lunch. I even missed the mindless tasks of sorting through drawers of cookware and stacking towels in the bathroom closet.

I compensated by cutting back on the time allocated for client lunches and sit-down conversations. I replaced them with telephone calls from the office. I also kept a sharper eye on the clock and tried to start home by four at the latest. Despite my best efforts, I seldom arrived home before six. That fall when the days grew short, I didn't make it home for a lot of the important things. It's funny, but small things that had no part in my previous life suddenly seemed important. A new calf was born, Felix found a supposedly authentic Indian arrowhead and Violet had a playmate come to visit after school. I missed all of these things, but that was simply part and parcel of being a working mother, wasn't it?

ON THANKSGIVING DAY I WAS out of bed before dawn, and by the time William and the kids sat down to breakfast I had a twenty-four pound turkey stuffed and in the oven.

When we sat down to dinner that afternoon, there were twelve of us gathered at the table: our family of four, Ophelia, Margaret, William's parents and the Lundmanns along with their two girls. Ed and Sally Lundmann were our next-door neighbors, so to speak, even though "next door" was a quarter mile down the road.

Before we ate, William said the blessing and thanked God for both a bountiful harvest and his new family.

"Amen to that," Ophelia said and gave me a wink.

When we were all so full we couldn't eat another bite, we played games, told stories and spoke of all we had to be thankful for.

"I'm thankful for getting to ride on a tractor," Felix said.

Violet rolled her eyes in typical big-sister fashion then stated she was thankful for having her own room and a new canopy bed.

The Lundmann girls were both thankful they now had neighbors to play with.

"And I'd be more thankful if I had a canopy bed too," the younger one added.

LATER THAT EVENING AFTER THE kids had brushed their teeth, said their prayers and fallen exhaustedly into bed, William and I sat side by side on the living room sofa.

"Did you ever dream our life together would be this good?" he asked.

I smiled at the thought and confessed that I didn't.

"I thought we'd be good together, but this…" I lifted his hand to my mouth and dropped a kiss into his palm. "I never knew something this good even existed."

We talked for a long time that night, and for the first time in many, many years I opened my soul and let the truth of my life spill out. Until then I had not spoken of the feelings I'd kept hidden for so long. I'd told the facts and spoken of the events but never the feelings. Alone I'd battled my way through hard times by keeping my heart hardened; I swallowed back the bitterness of loss and stood my ground. I did what I had to do because I was the only one I could count on. I was the only one the kids could count on. Now it was different. William and I were so much more than a man and woman sleeping together; we were a family.

That night when the moon was high in the sky and everyone else fast asleep, William and I made love. Afterward he held me in his arms and I knew that for as long as we lived our souls would be intertwined, one to the other.

❀

A WEEK BEFORE CHRISTMAS I was in the kitchen fixing breakfast when a sudden bout of nausea overcame me. I ran for the bathroom, threw up my morning coffee and was still nauseous. My first thought was I'd had too many of the cookies we'd been baking, but when I threw up a second time I suspected otherwise.

I washed my face, forced down a piece of dry toast and then left for work. On the way home that evening I stopped at the drugstore and bought a pregnancy test. I waited until after the kids were in bed then slipped into the bathroom. The stick turned blue.

Hopefully William will see this as good news, I thought.

He was sitting on the sofa watching a basketball game. I walked in and dropped down beside him.

Without thinking about it, he reached across and laid his hand on my thigh.

"How was your day?" he asked.

"Eventful," I answered.

He turned to me. "Eventful? In what way?"

I gave him the whole story of how I had been sick this morning, and when I got to the part where the stick turned blue he broke out in the happiest smile I've ever seen. I didn't have to wonder if he was pleased with the news; the answer was in his smile.

"So we're having a baby," he said. "Wow, imagine me having a baby."

I laughed. "Actually I'll be doing all the heavy lifting on this one, but I'm definitely going to need a birthing coach."

"I'll be there," he swore. "Every minute, every second."

He kissed my mouth as tenderly as you'd kiss a sleeping infant, and I was filled with the joy of knowing this baby would have a loving father.

THAT NIGHT I DREAMT OF my own daddy. I saw him up in heaven smiling down at me.

"This is good," he said and gathered me into his arms the way he used to do. When the dream ended I could still feel Daddy's arms around me, but once I opened my eyes I realized it was William who had snuggled close during the night.

I usually jump out of bed as soon as my eyes are open, but I didn't that morning. I stayed there for another ten minutes just to enjoy the good feeling I had in my heart.

DILLY BEANS

That week William chopped down a pine, and we decorated it with colored lights and ornaments of every shape and size. I had never seen the kids as excited as they were that year. They hung decorations in every room of the house: snowflake cutouts, hand-drawn angels, paper chains. Glitter sparkles were everywhere, even stuck to little hands and noses.

On Christmas Eve we went to church as a family. Not since before Daddy died had I felt so loved and complete. As I sat in the pew listening to the choir sing of that holy night I understood how it felt to be Mary, not as the mother of the Christ Child but as the mother of a baby who would be born into a world of love and adoration.

THEY SAY TIME WAITS FOR no one, and it's true. It hurries by whether you want it to or not. That holiday season was so filled with laughter and happiness I wished it could last forever, but it came and went in the blink of an eye. Christmas Day was a frantic flurry of ribbons, wrapping paper and squeals of excitement. Our living room was cluttered with new dolls, toy trucks and even a sled.

I'd laughed at William when he brought the sled home.

"We get very little snow in Virginia," I said. "Why buy a sled?"

He'd shrugged. "Felix had it on his list."

As fate would have it, we had a seven-inch snowfall in the second week of January. School was canceled, and William took the kids sledding on the hill behind the orchard. I was back at work by then and with the slick roads didn't get home until almost eight.

When I came in, Felix ran to greet me.

"Mama," he shouted, "guess what? We had snow, and Daddy took us sledding!" By then both kids had begun to call William Daddy.

"That's wonderful," I said, a bit jealous that I hadn't been home for such an event.

"I was great!" Felix said.

"I was great too," Violet added, but not quite as enthusiastically.

Their comments were reflective of their personalities. Felix is my little fireball, Violet as soft and lovely as her name.

THAT WINTER VIRGINIA HAD MORE than its share of freezing rain, snow and ice. Driving back and forth to Wyattsville was slow and at times treacherous. More than once William suggested I not go to work, but I did nonetheless. I figured with the baby due in July I'd be taking most of August off, and that was enough.

THE FIRST NOTICE CAME IN late February. It was a short and simple e-mail sent to everyone who worked for the *Tribune*. The message said that Drummond-Hill, a Richmond-based publisher, had purchased the paper. While there would be some minor restructuring in the coming months, for now we were to continue operations as they were.

That afternoon the office was abuzz with speculation as to what might happen. Gloria felt sure it meant the end of our jobs. John Willoughby thought it might be a good time to ask for a raise because they'd be looking to keep productive workers on the team. Ernie, a man who'd worked for the *Tribune* for thirty years, claimed it was a death knell.

"We'll all be gone by summer," he said, then added that he was going to go ahead and put in for retirement before they changed the structuring there also.

Everything was up in the air. I was one of the top producers so I felt reasonably sure my job was safe, but there was no guarantee.

That night after the kids were in bed, I told William about the e-mail.

"Rumor has it that there could be some layoffs coming," I said.

"Wouldn't be the worst thing in the world," he replied. "We'd manage."

"I don't think they would let me go," I said, "but there are plenty of others…"

"Oh," he said with disappointment in his voice.

ON MARCH FIFTEENTH THE FIRST round of layoffs started. Instead of starting at the bottom, they started at the top. When everyone arrived that Monday morning, Willard Moss, the advertising manager, was gone. His nameplate had been removed from the holder outside his office and replaced with that of Franklin Priest, a man no one had ever heard of before. Before the day had ended Mister Priest had called four supervisors and six clerical employees into his office, handed them their severance checks and told them their services were no longer required.

After that nothing was the same around the office. There were no water cooler conversations, and few people took time to sit in the lounge for a coffee break.

The second round of layoffs came April first, and then on April fifteenth I was cut.

"We're eliminating the commission-based sales structure," Mister Priest said. He rattled on with a lengthy explanation of how they appreciated my past performance but of necessity had to move in the direction best suited for the company.

That evening when I told William his mouth curled into a grin.

"Good," he said. "It'll be nice to have you at home."

"But the money…"

"Don't worry," he said. "We'll manage just fine."

Not worrying was a new concept for me, but it settled into my head quite comfortably and I began to look forward to a nice long summer vacation. I had a good track record, so I could always get another job. In the fall I'd start looking after the baby was born, after I'd had myself a good long rest and plenty of time to enjoy my growing family.

BY THEN THE LUNDMANN GIRLS had become fast friends with Violet and Felix, and once school was out they were constant visitors at our house. At first Sally would drive by and drop them off, but once she discovered I was no longer working she stayed for coffee and conversation. In the middle of June she came in lugging a bushel basket of green beans.

"We had a bumper harvest this year," she said, "and I thought maybe you'd like to can some dilly beans."

The whole dilly bean thing was new to me. I had never in my

life canned anything. I had always been a working woman, a woman who bought things already cooked and in cans.

I told Sally this, and she laughed out loud then hauled me off for a shopping spree. That afternoon she and I came home with three dozen mason jars, a book on canning and an armload of spices. Together we pickled all those beans and packed them into sealed jars.

A week later I asked William to build some extra shelves in the pantry because I was planning to do blackberries, peaches and strawberries.

That summer I did all the things I'd never had time to do. I walked through the fields with Violet. I watched Felix climb onto the tractor and sit on William's lap. I sat on the back porch and ate lunch with William, and some afternoons I drove over to visit Ophelia.

I enjoyed every minute of my time and my pregnancy. On lazy afternoons I would sit in the front porch swing and push myself back and forth. All the while I'd keep one hand on my tummy waiting for Eugene to kick or move around. By then we knew I was having a boy and planned to name him after the grandpa who inspired William's love of farming.

I talked to this baby just as I had Baby Girl. With a gentle nudge of my foot I'd set the swing in motion and then sit there making up rhyming songs with his name.

"Eugene, dilly bean, lots of things I've never seen. You'll be baby number three, and you will have a family..."

Eugene was born on the first Tuesday of July. He came into this world with a healthy set of lungs and the same blue eyes as Violet and Felix.

Summer was like being on vacation, a vacation that gave me time to be a real wife and mother. In the early morning I sat in the rocking chair with Eugene at my breast and no thought of having to be here, there or anywhere. In the afternoon when the sun warmed the ground and a breeze rippled across the fields, I'd strap Eugene to my chest and take all three children on an adventure. We tromped across fields of corn, picked berries and one afternoon we even petted a cow. Funny how the memory of Felix doing that stands out in my memory. He giggled and laughed so hard Violet and I were soon chuckling along with him.

It was a wonderful summer, but it was a vacation. Vacations are not meant to last. I knew that with the coming of fall it would be time to start looking for another job.

Perceived Value

A person can measure their self-worth by any number of ways. For some it is based on popularity; others weigh it on a scale of beauty or creativity or wealth. But regardless of how it is measured, the validation of a person's worth always comes from outside, never inside. It comes in the form of accolades, titles, trophies or awards. It is something counted up and given to you as an acknowledgement of that worth. After so many years of being the breadwinner, I'd been conditioned to measure my worth by the amount in my paycheck.

I'd started as the new kid in Classifieds and worked my way up to district manager. Each step up had been the result of long hours and hard work. I was the one who could be counted on to pull the loose ends together and make things happen. It was challenging and exciting. Taking the summer off for a nice long vacation had been fun, but now with Felix and Violet back in school it was time for me to find a job.

When I first mentioned this to William, he looked at me with a puzzled expression, scratched his head and asked, "Why?"

"Because I miss working, and we can use the extra income."

William walked past me and started washing his hands at the

kitchen sink. When he has a different point of view he takes his sweet old time getting to what it is he wants to say.

He dried his hands on a paper towel then said, "You haven't worked all summer, and we've managed just fine. The bills are paid, and there's some left over."

"Maybe so," I said. "But wouldn't it be nice to have a bit more?"

He gave a careless shrug. "It's not something we really need."

"We don't need pie either," I said, "but it's nice to have." With that I turned away and dropped the subject.

It had been the plan all along. I would take the summer off, have the baby and return to work in the fall. It's what I'd always done, so why would we change things now? The extra income would mean we could splurge on luxuries, do things we might not otherwise do.

A week passed and William said nothing more. I figured he'd come to grips with the thought of my returning to work, so I updated my resume and started a job search.

After so many years of working in the field, I knew several companies in the area and sent my resume to all of them. I also picked through the newspaper ads and pulled a few more leads. Then I called some of my old *Tribune* clients and asked if they knew of any openings.

Dawn Hawkins at Travel-Pro referred me to Penn and Penn, and Henry Travis, a vice president at the bank, said he knew for sure the Yellow Pages Directory in Taunton was looking for a field sales rep.

I sent resumes to both and got interviews with both.

With the older children in school and William busy with harvest, it was easy enough to manage. I dropped Eugene off at Ophelia's then continued on to my interviews.

The Yellow Pages position was a managerial spot covering the entire western region of Virginia. The pay was good, but the travel demands were huge. With three kids and a husband to take care of, I wouldn't be able to manage it. Thanking them for their time, I bowed out.

Penn and Penn turned out to be a mid-sized ad agency looking for a new business development manager. I'd always enjoyed the challenge of creating a clientele I could call my own; it's what I did best. Plus the agency was located in Middleboro, which was only two towns over from Burnsville, and I could set my own schedule.

"We're looking for someone who can focus on production numbers, not punch a time clock," the human resources manager said.

"That's right up my alley," I replied and told her of how I'd more than doubled my client base at the *Tribune*.

We spoke for nearly an hour; then she said, "I like your qualifications. I'd like to arrange a meeting with our managing partner and get back to you."

Three days later she called and invited me back for a second interview.

"Mister Penn is interested in speaking with you," she said.

MY INTERVIEW WITH CHARLES PENN turned out to be far more challenging than the first one. He wanted to know how I had gone about identifying and approaching new customers. He asked for sales numbers and also inquired as to whether having children would interfere with my work schedule.

"I had two young babies when I was working at the *Tribune*, and it never interfered," I said. "Eugene, like my first two babies, will be in daycare, so I see no conflict."

We then spoke about salary, and there was a sizable gap in what I wanted and what he was offering. I'd asked for $65,000; he was offering $55,000.

"But bear in mind," he said, "you'll get ten percent commission on all the business you bring in. If you're as good as you say you are, you can develop enough new business to take you up to seventy-five thousand easily."

As we went back and forth, he continued to scribble notes in the margin of my resume.

"And assuming you get this position," he said, "when would you be able to start?"

"Right away," I answered.

He added one last note in the margin then stood signifying the meeting was over.

"I'd like to discuss this with my partner and get back to you," he said. "But I think it's fair to say we're interested; very interested."

A WEEK PASSED BEFORE HIS secretary called and said Mister Penn would like to see me again. We set up an appointment for the following Monday.

That afternoon I filled William in on everything.

"I'm almost positive they're going to make me an offer," I said.

Maybe I should have noticed his lack of enthusiasm, but I didn't. He moved past me without even a sideways glance and lifted Eugene from his bouncy seat. Talking to the baby, not me, he said, "Why don't you tell your mama to forget about working and stay home with you?"

Eugene squealed happily and I laughed, thinking it nothing more than baby-talk conversation.

Over the years I had become a person with set-in-stone goals. I had to be. I was alone and had a family to provide for. At that moment I was focused on the horizon, on getting the job, on the potential for making more money than ever before. I was blinded by my own vision and couldn't see what was right there beside me. William was talking, but I wasn't listening.

THE WEEKEND BEFORE WHAT WOULD be my third interview, I was a nervous wreck. I had a headache, and my stomach felt like I'd just stepped off of a rollercoaster. It didn't help that William was downright testy with me, and any time I so much as mentioned the job or the interview he got up and left the room.

On Sunday it poured rain, and we were all stuck in the house. Eugene had a tooth trying to break through and was fussy all afternoon. He wasn't happy in his bouncy seat and continued to wail even after I put him in the baby carrier and strapped it to my chest. Violet and Felix got into an argument over nothing and after a considerable amount of shouting got sent to their rooms. Regardless of what I said or didn't say, William continued to act miffed. None of this helped my nervous stomach.

Monday morning I woke up so nauseous I could barely hold my head up. The interview was at eleven, so I got the kids off to school, then took a shower and tried to get myself moving. William didn't even wait for me to make him breakfast; he had a cup of coffee and left.

I dropped Eugene off at Ophelia's then headed for Middleboro. Halfway there I had to pull off the road. I got out, walked around to the other side of the car and threw up. That's when I began to suspect it wasn't just a nervous stomach.

MY MEETING WITH CHARLES PENN went just as I'd guessed. They made me the offer but stayed at $55,000, plus commissions. I'd been in business long enough to know how to play the game, so I said I thought I was worth more and I needed a day or so to think it over.

"That sounds fair," Penn said, "but just keep in mind that the potential here means you'll probably be making in excess of seventy-five thousand."

I assured him I would take that into consideration. The truth was I already knew I was going to accept the job; it was perfect for me. But with William acting as he had been, I thought it best that we sit down and have an actual discussion about it. Not speaking to one another wasn't working too well in my book.

On the way home from the interview I stopped and bought another pregnancy test. I almost didn't need one because the symptoms had become so familiar that I already knew what the result would be.

You might think the thought of another baby would be enough to dissuade me from taking the job, but it wasn't. I would do as I had always done: work up until the last week, have the baby, take a month off and then return to work.

THAT EVENING I WAITED UNTIL Violet and Felix were in bed; then I sat on the sofa beside William.

"We need to talk," I said.

"About what?" he answered.

"Penn and Penn offered me the job." I explained what a great opportunity it was and all the money I'd be making.

"I'm really good with new business development," I told him. "So there's a strong possibility I'd make more than seventy-five thousand."

"You're also good at being a wife and mother," he said, "and that's worth way more than seventy-five thousand."

I wasn't sure whether to thank him for the compliment or argue that being a mother didn't put money in our bank account. I didn't have a chance to do either.

"They think you're worth seventy-five thousand," William went on, "but let's take a look at what you're worth to me and our family. Good quality childcare with someone giving the kids the love and attention you give them would easily run forty thousand a child; that's a hundred-and-twenty thousand right there. Then add in the cost of a driver to pick them up and drop them off for play dates, doctor visits, soccer practice and the like; that's another fifty thousand."

He stood, snapped the television off and continued. "Oh, and now that we've gotten used to the great meals you make we'll need a gourmet chef, so that's another eighty or ninety thousand. Plus we'll need a bookkeeper to pay bills and keep my records straight, so that's another fifty thousand. And it will cost us another twenty thousand or so to have a tutor come in and help the kids with their homework."

He ticked the numbers off on his fingers and said, "We're already up to three hundred-and-thirty thousand, and I haven't even added in the value of having you close by when I come in from the field."

He turned, gave a smile that made my heart melt and pulled me into his arms. With his eyes locked on mine he said, "That's worth way more than a million." He pressed his strong hand against my back and pulled me closer.

"So they're only offering you a paltry fifty-five thousand, but we think you're worth a million-and-a-half."

Before I could speak he bent and covered my mouth with his.

With the moon full, the kids sleeping and the air filled with the sweet smell of the harvest, we made love. Afterward as we lay locked in an embrace, I whispered in his ear, "I think you've got to add an additional forty thousand to your number."

He twisted his neck and peered at me sideways. "Why?"

"We're having another baby."

THE BIG PICTURE

Years earlier when I was still a girl, the school had a class trip to the Virginia Museum of Fine Art. I came across a painting called *A Mandolin Player* by William Merritt Chase. I was so entranced by the blend of colors that I stood only inches away from the painting studying every tiny little brush stroke. I'd been there ten, maybe fifteen minutes when an elderly gentleman who was curled over and leaning heavily on his cane tapped me on the shoulder.

"Move back," he said.

He'd startled me so I turned. "Excuse me?"

"Move back," he repeated. "When you're too close you focus on the details but miss the beauty of the picture."

I moved back and sat on the bench. He hobbled over and sat beside me.

I smiled at him and said, "You're right. Now I can see how everything blends and comes together. It's more beautiful than I thought."

The old man nodded. "I know. But it takes a lot of years before you learn to look at things that way."

After what William had said, I knew I'd been looking at just the brush strokes of our life. I hadn't taken time to step back and see the beauty of the picture.

LATER THAT AFTERNOON, I CALLED Charles Penn and told him I had decided to decline his offer.

"Family obligations," I explained.

It took him a few moments to respond; then he said, "You got a better offer, didn't you?"

I laughed. "Yes, I suppose I did."

"Tell me how much," he said. "I'll match it."

"I don't think so," I replied. "It's upwards of a million-and-a-half."

"Seriously?"

"Yes, seriously."

ELEANOR WAS BORN IN EARLY June. By then I had settled into a routine that was easy to love. With two babies, two more in school and a husband who enjoyed coming in to have lunch with us, I wondered how I had ever managed both a career and motherhood.

One day when I playfully strapped Eugene in his carrier on my back and Eleanor in her infant carrier to my chest, William snapped a picture of me. When I looked at it and saw the smiles of myself and both babies, I knew I'd managed but had never taken the time to enjoy every moment as I was doing now.

THREE MONTHS AFTER ELEANOR'S BIRTH the telephone rang in the middle of the afternoon, and when I answered it was William calling from his cell phone.

"Cheryl Ann," he said, "there's something we need to talk about."

Him telephoning me in the middle of the day was unusual to say the least, so I asked, "Where are you?"

"In the barn," he answered. "I've got something troubling my mind and—"

"Can we talk about it later?" I said. "I've got Eleanor in the bath."

"Okay. But let's just make sure we do."

His voice was as serious as I've ever heard, and I started wondering what in the world could be troubling him. I wasn't pregnant, and I'd completely given up any thought of a job.

Oh, no. Maybe that's it. Maybe we actually need the money and he's going to ask me to go back to work.

That thought weighed down my heart like a two-ton brick. I worried all afternoon but couldn't come up with any other possibility. I called him back, but there was no answer.

BY THE TIME WILLIAM CAME in that afternoon, Violet and Felix were home from school, Eugene was up from his nap, Eleanor was in her bouncy chair and I was starting a stew for dinner. I was standing at the stove adding vegetables to the pot when he passed by and kissed me on the back of my neck.

"What did you want to talk about?" I asked nervously.

"It can wait until after dinner," he said and went into the mudroom where he could wash up. "Smells good!" he hollered.

I was totally bewildered. Earlier his voice had such intensity, but now it was soft and easy sounding. I began to think maybe it wasn't money, because he didn't look one bit worried. I put the lid on the pot and followed him into the mudroom.

"What did you want to talk about?" I asked again.

He kissed the side of my face and whispered, "I'll tell you later, after the kids go to bed."

Our family had no secrets. We spoke openly and in front of the children. So I couldn't begin to guess what was on his mind. Not knowing is far worse than knowing, because regardless of the situation you imagine the worst.

I turned the fire up under the stew and had it bubbling away in a matter of minutes. Dinner was on the table a full half-hour earlier than usual. Immediately after dinner, Violet and Felix were herded into their routines of tooth brushing and bedtime prayers.

"It's not bedtime yet," Felix complained.

"That's okay," I said. "It's been a long day, and you're tired."

"I'm not tired," Felix argued.

"Yes, you are." I kissed him goodnight and snapped off the light.

By then Eugene was already asleep in his crib.

The last one down was Eleanor. Her I couldn't rush. I sat in the rocker, held her to my breast and waited until she was satisfied and sleepy. Once Eleanor was in her crib with the blanket tucked around her, I joined William in the living room.

I sat next to him and said, "Now, what was so horrible that you couldn't talk about it in front of the children?"

He gave me a wide-eyed look of surprise. "It's not horrible at all! In fact I think it'll be good."

"What will be good?"

He snapped off the television, gave a deep sigh and leaned back against the sofa. "Well, I've been thinking about the kids. It doesn't seem right that I'm a real daddy to two of them and not the other two…"

I sat there waiting.

"But if you and I adopted Violet and Felix, then we'd be a whole family."

This was not something we'd spoken of before, not something I'd ever asked of him.

"You want to adopt Violet and Felix?" I echoed.

He gave me a big grin and nodded. "You said their birth daddies aren't interested in being part of their life, and I think they ought to have a daddy the same as Eugene and Eleanor."

"You know what I think...?" I drew the words out and left the question hanging.

He looked a bit puzzled. "No, what do you think?"

"I think I married the most wonderful man in the entire world!" I threw my arms around his neck and kissed him so hard I almost broke a tooth.

YOU MIGHT THINK THAT SINCE neither of the fathers wanted their babies it would have been an easy slam-dunk, but it wasn't. Even though they'd both walked away and not once looked back, I had to track Nick and Vince down and get them to sign a release saying it was okay for William to adopt their unwanted children.

NICK WAS EASIER THAN VINCE. The gas station Nick had worked for was torn down years ago, but I remembered Herb had said Nick moved back to Baltimore. That's where I started. There were nineteen Nicholas Lombardis in Baltimore. The one I was searching for was number twelve.

I explained that I had gotten married and my husband wanted to adopt Violet.

"He's already like her father," I said, "but we wanted to make it official."

"How is she?" Nick asked wistfully.

I started to say "Good," but then I changed it. "No, actually, she's great. Smart and beautiful and —"

"Okay," he cut in. "Send me the paperwork."

VINCE WAS FAR MORE DIFFICULT. I remembered his last name was Dougherty and that he came from somewhere in the Wyattsville area. I searched the Richmond County phone book and three surrounding counties and came up with four Vince Doughertys, none of which were him.

I backtracked the connections of that night. He had been a friend of Amy Elkins, but even back then I'd only known her in passing. I searched the telephone directory then called A. Elkins, A.R. Elkins and Amie Elkins. None of them were her.

I called Nicole. "Do you remember that girl, Amy Elkins? She was at the Horsehead the night of that party?"

Nicole chuckled. "Good grief, that was almost nine years ago!"

"Yes, I know," I said. I explained about William wanting to adopt Violet and Felix. "The thing is I need to get a signed release from Vince, the guy that..."

"Yeah, I know who you mean."

Following our conversation, Nicole made several phone calls and got back to me a few days later.

"I found Amy," she said. "She gave me Vince's cell phone number. She wasn't sure if he still had the same number but thought so."

THAT AFTERNOON I CALLED THE number Nicole had given me. The phone rang twice and then was redirected into voicemail.

"I'm not available," the voice said. "Leave a message."

There was no mention of his name.

"Hi," I stammered. "I'm trying to reach Vince Dougherty. My

name is Cheryl Ann McLeod. If you could call me back I'd appreciate it." I rattled off my telephone number and hung up.

Two days later I got a call back.

"Cheryl Ann?" he said. "This is Vincent Dougherty. You left a message on my phone?"

"Yes," I said anxiously. "Thank you so much for calling." I launched into a jittery explanation of how McLeod was my married name, and he most likely remembered me as Cheryl Ann Ferguson.

Sounding somewhat bewildered he said, "Do I know you?"

"It's been a while," I said. "Almost nine years, but we were together after that party at the Horsehead—"

"Nine years? What party?"

I backed up and went step by step through the whole sorrowful mess, explaining how I'd had a baby and spoken to him afterward asking whether he wanted to be involved in his son's life.

"Are you looking for money or something? Because if you are—"

"I am not looking for money," I said emphatically. "I'm married now, and my husband would like to adopt Felix legally. All I want from you is a release stating that you've given your consent to the adoption."

"I don't even remember you, and I'm not gonna sign something saying he's my kid. I sign a paper like that, then you come back looking for money. Is that the game?"

"No game," I said. "All I want is for my husband to be able to legally adopt Felix."

"I don't know," he grumbled. "I don't feel good about doing this."

I begged and pleaded. Finally he said that if I would first send him a notarized statement saying he was in no way financially responsible, he'd consider signing the release.

"But," he said, "I've got to get that notarized letter from you first."

I took down his address and said I would send it. When I hung up the phone, I stood there shaking. I felt so stupid and ashamed of myself. How could I have ever let such a man touch me? I carried his baby for nine months, suffered through the agony of childbirth and raised the child he fathered, yet he didn't even remember my name. I cried for well over an hour, not because of Vince but because of my own shame.

That night after the kids were in bed, I sat beside William and told him of the conversation. He listened with his head bowed, his forearms resting on his thighs and his hands dropped down between his knees. I told him of my shame and cried again. When I finished the story he took me in his arms and held my head against his chest.

"That's behind you," he said. "Let's not waste time looking behind us; let's look ahead to the future."

IT TOOK ALMOST SIX MONTHS before we got both releases and filed the adoption papers. The day the court gave us their stamp of approval, our whole family celebrated with root beer floats.

We celebrated because we truly were a family now.

The Legacy

Two months after the adoptions were finalized, I received an envelope in the mail. I recognized the return address in Lawton and tore it open immediately.

There were three things in the envelope: a note from LeAnn, a picture and a newspaper clipping.

I am so proud of our girl, LeAnn wrote, *and I know you will be also. A week from Friday is her high school graduation. She has been named valedictorian and will be giving the keynote address. Dean and I will both be attending the ceremony, and although I have only two tickets for the seating area if you slip into the back gallery after the program has started you can listen to what she has to say.*

I hope these past years have been kind to you. God knows ours have been truly wonderful because of your great generosity.

We are and will continue to be eternally grateful.

Love, LeAnn

I HELD THE PICTURE AND studied the face. It was Morgan, but if you tilted your head one way or the other you could have believed it was me when I was her age. She had the same eyes, the same curve of her chin, the same smile.

Her hair hung down in loose ripples, just as mine did.

Morgan was almost the same age I was when I left Spruce Street. I thought about that year and wondered if back then I had ever been so young and innocent looking. She was Ryan's daughter but had none of his features. She was all me. Me, young and hopeful. Me, starry-eyed and looking forward to the future.

I set the picture aside and read the newspaper clipping. It referenced the upcoming graduation and said Morgan Stuart, daughter of Dean and LeAnn Stuart of Lawton, would be the keynote speaker.

ON FRIDAY, JUNE 6TH, WILLIAM was up long before dawn. He downed a quick cup of coffee and headed out to milk the cows, feed the chickens and attend to the chores that couldn't be put off for another day. It was almost one-thirty when he returned to the house.

"You'll have to hurry," I told him. "The ceremony starts at three."

He grabbed the sandwich I had waiting and headed for the shower. Sally Lundmann's car pulled into our driveway minutes later. She climbed out and hurried inside.

"Thank you so much for watching the children," I said. "Eugene and Eleanor are both napping, and the school bus will drop Violet and Felix off at the end of the driveway at two-fifteen."

I double-checked to make sure Sally had my cell phone number and told her to call if there was any problem. She assured me everything would be fine.

"Stop worrying," she said. "Just go and enjoy yourself."

I am not a person with secrets. There are many things in my past that perhaps should have been kept secret, but they were not.

Secrets are only a hair's breadth away from lies, and in my lifetime I had already witnessed more than enough lies.

Sally knew about Morgan, just as William and the children knew. I had always hoped that one day my Baby Girl would come in search of me. If or when she did, our door would be thrown open wide and I would wrap my arms around her. She would meet the brothers and sisters who for so many years had heard the mention of her name.

I know we will never be her family. She has a family, a family who adores her. It is as it should be. I am content to simply be her birth mother, the woman who brought her into this world. My first child may never find a place in her heart for me, but I will forever hold her in mine.

THE CEREMONY WAS UNDERWAY WHEN William and I quietly slipped through the auditorium doors and stood in the back corner. We anxiously waited through three other speeches before Morgan was introduced.

"Now, ladies and gentlemen, honored guests and faculty, please allow me to introduce our next speaker and the Class valedictorian, Morgan Stuart."

A round of applause with cheering and foot stamping followed the introduction.

"Go for it, Morgan!" one of the students in the audience shouted.

She stepped to the microphone, poised and ready.

"Fellow graduates," she began, "over the past four years here at Lawton High we have learned a lot. Now, as we move forward into the world, we will discover how much more we have yet to learn..."

She spoke of the importance of relationships, the importance of community and how they, the students of today, were the building blocks of the future.

"Your success in this world will not be measured by the achievements of today," she said, "but how you handle the adversities of tomorrow. The achievements of today belong not to us but to those who have brought us to this moment. Our families, our teachers and the countless others who have lifted us up and spurred us on."

She glanced down at a group of parents sitting in the audience. "We all have people to thank, I perhaps more than anyone."

Her voice was strong and filled with compassion. She had my face, but her ways and movements were those of LeAnn.

"We all thank our mothers and fathers," she said, "but I have two mothers to thank. Before I was born my birth mother selected my family for me. She chose a father and mother who would love me, care for me, nurture me and bring me to where I am today. My birth mother faced an overwhelming amount of adversity, but she loved me enough to give me a childhood free of those things. I hope to become just such a woman: a woman who can rise above what is and see the future of what can be."

She lifted her face and looked out into the audience, and for a brief moment I wondered if perhaps she knew I was there. If she had somehow spotted the face that was an older version of her own.

"And so, my fellow graduates, as we leave Lawton High and begin the next phase of our life, we carry with us the memories of what was, but let us also stand ready to build a future for those who follow in our footsteps."

I pulled a tissue from my pocket and wiped away the tears rolling down my cheeks. When the principal stepped to the podium and began to give his closing remarks, William and I slipped out the door.

As we crossed the campus heading back to the parking lot, William wrapped his arm around my waist and snuggled me close.

"Cheryl Ann," he said, "have I ever told you how very proud I am of you?"

I looked up at him and smiled. "Possibly. But I wouldn't mind hearing it again."

I ONCE THOUGHT MY GREATEST achievement in life was simply surviving. Now I look back and realize how foolish such a thought was. A person's worth cannot be judged by the amount of money they make or the things they own. A person's worth can only be measured by the value they have passed along to others.

I am older now and wiser. I see my five beautiful children and know they are a legacy that will stretch far beyond my years.

Yes, I include Morgan as one of mine, because in my heart she still is, and will always be, my Baby Girl.

If you enjoyed reading this book, please post a review at your favorite on-line retailer and share your thoughts with other readers.

I'd love to hear from you. If you visit my website and sign up to receive my monthly newsletter, as a special thank you, you'll receive a copy of
A HOME IN HOPEFUL

http://betteleecrosby.com

Baby Girl is Book Four in the Memory House Series.

Turn the page for a peek inside the other Memory House Books.

MEMORY HOUSE

The Memory House Series, Book One

Annie Cross is running from a broken love affair when she stops at the tiny bed and breakfast inn. She is looking to forget the past, but what she finds is a future filled with the magic of lost memories. A heartwarming story of love and friendship. Winner of a FPA President's Book Award Silver Medal.

THE LOFT

The Memory House Series, Book Two

Fifty years of memories are hidden in the walls of the loft. Now Ophelia Browne is leaving the house and she's leaving some very powerful memories behind. Annie needs to find just one...the one that will save Oliver's life. A story of believing in miracles and the power of love.

WHAT THE HEART REMEMBERS

The Memory House Series, Book Three

Two lovers, one chance at happiness....When Max Martinelli returns to Paris in search of her lost love, what she finds will change her life forever. For three years the memory of Julien Marceau has haunted Max. Her life is stuck on hold simply because she can't stop wondering what would have happened if she had gone back.

Spare Change
The Wyattsville Series, Book One

Winner of five Literary Awards, *Spare Change* has been compared to John Grisham's *The Client*. Eleven-year-old Ethan Allen Doyle has witnessed a brutal murder and now the boy is running for his life. Olivia Westerly is the only person he can trust, and he's not too sure he can trust her. She's got no love of children and a truckload of superstitions—one of them is the belief that eleven is the unluckiest number on earth.

Jubilee's Journey
The Wyattsville Series, Book Two

Winner of the 2014 FPA President's Book Award Gold Medal, *Jubilee's Journey* is the story of a child born in the West Virginia mountains and orphaned before she is seven. When she and her older brother go in search of an aunt, he is caught up in a crime not of his making. Jubilee knows the truth, but who is going to believe a seven-year-old child?

Passing Through Perfect
The Wyattsville Series, Book Three

Passing through Perfect is a story rife with the injustices of the South and rich with the compassion of strangers. It's 1946. The war is over. Millions of American soldiers are coming home and Benjamin Church is one of them. After four years of being away he thought things in Alabama would have changed, but they haven't. Grinder's Corner is as it's always been—a hardscrabble burp in the road. It's not much, but it's home.

THE TWELFTH CHILD
The Serendipity Series, Book One

The Twelfth Child is an uplifting tale of trust, love and friendship. To escape a planned marriage, a willful daughter leaves home and makes her way in a Depression-era world. When she is nearing the tail end of her years, she meets the young woman with whom she forges a friendship that lasts beyond life.

PREVIOUSLY LOVED TREASURES
The Serendipity Series, Book Two

Previously Loved Treasures is a story that resonates with heartwarming albeit quirky characters and the joy of a pay-it-forward philosophy. When Ida Sweetwater opens a rooming house, she will find the granddaughter she never knew she had and turn a group of haphazard strangers into a family.

WISHING FOR WONDERFUL
The Serendipity Series, Book Three

Wishing for Wonderful is a story narrated by a Cupid with attitude. It will have you laughing out loud as Cupid uses a homeless dog in his scheme to give two deserving couples the love they deserve.

CRACKS IN THE SIDEWALK

A *USA Today* Bestseller and Winner of the 2014 Reader's Favorite Gold Medal, *Cracks in the Sidewalk* is a powerful family saga that is a heartrending reminder of how fragile relationships can be. Based on the true story of a woman's search for her missing grandchildren.

WHAT MATTERS MOST

In *What Matters Most* Louise Palmer is faced with life-altering changes and must choose between friendships and marriage. Although it is at times laugh-out-loud funny, beneath the humor there is a message of love, tolerance and coming to grips with reality.

BLUEBERRY HILL

Blueberry Hill asks the poignant question—can love save a person from self-destruction? In a heartrending memoir Crosby looks back to a time when the sisters were young enough to feel invincible and foolish enough to believe it would last forever.

A Note from the Author

For I know the plans I have for you declares The Lord…
Plans to prosper you and not to harm you.
Plans to give you hope and a future.
Jeremiah 29:11

This verse from Jeremiah hangs on the wall of my office, and it is particularly apt for this story. Writing a novel is never an easy task. Writing one that delves into the most painful aspects of a person's life is unbelievably difficult.

Long before I began writing this novel, a woman named Crystal shared her own story with me. It was a story much like Cheryl's and touched my heart with such poignancy that I simply couldn't set it aside. We talked about the heartache of being a forgotten birth mother, and she graciously said, "When you're ready to write this story, I will tell you all of mine." She did, and that story became the inspiration for *Baby Girl*. I will forever be grateful to Crystal J. Casavant Otto for opening up the painful past and sharing her story of trial and triumph.

I also want to thank the people who are the constants in my life, those who inspire me and help me to make each new book a reality.

I thank my friend, Joanne Bliven, for being the best story consultant ever. When my characters paint themselves into a corner, Joanne and I open a bottle of wine and talk it through. Trust me, it is always easier to find your way out of a predicament when you have a friend who is willing to listen. This is true in life as well as fiction.

I thank my husband, Richard, for being my biggest fan and supporting me in more ways than I can count...not the least of which is reading through a manuscript when he'd much rather be watching a football game. Dick is not only my husband; he is also my sweetheart and my greatest blessing.

I thank my editor, Ekta Garg, for polishing and perfecting my stories. Without Ekta, I would forever be bogged down in the strategy of commas.

And I would be sorely remiss if I did not thank the Bent Pine Publicity Director, Coral Russell, for things too numerous to mention. I am constantly telling her she is a genius, and that's pretty much how I feel. I am blessed to be working with Coral, for ours is more than a business relationship. It is a true friendship.

Last but not least, I thank the loyal fans and followers who buy my books, share them with friends and take time to write a review. Without these wonderful readers, my stories would be all too soon forgotten.

About the Author

AWARD-WINNING NOVELIST BETTE LEE CROSBY brings the wit and wisdom of her Southern Mama to works of fiction—the result is a delightful blend of humor, mystery and romance.

"Storytelling is in my blood," Crosby laughingly admits, "My mom was not a writer, but she was a captivating storyteller, so I find myself using bits and pieces of her voice in most everything I write."

Crosby's work was first recognized in 2006 when she received The National League of American Pen Women Award for a then unpublished manuscript. Since then, she has gone on to win numerous other awards, including The Reviewer's Choice Award, FPA President's Book Award Gold Medal and The Royal Palm Literary Award.

To learn more about Bette Lee Crosby, explore her other work, or read a sample from any of her books, visit her blog at:

http://betteleecrosby.com

Made in the USA
Monee, IL
24 August 2019